W9-BWX-611

LOVE THY NEIGHBOR

Center Point
Large Print

Also by Debbie Macomber and available from Center Point Large Print:

Twenty Wishes
Summer on Blossom Street
Bride on the Loose
Same Time, Next Year
Mail-Order Bride
Hannah's List
Turn in the Road
Girl Like Janet

**This Large Print Book carries the
Seal of Approval of N.A.V.H.**

LOVE THY NEIGHBOR

Debbie Macomber

CENTER POINT LARGE PRINT
THORNDIKE, MAINE

This Center Point Large Print edition is published
in the year 2012 by arrangement with
Debbie Macomber, Inc.

The text of this Large Print edition is unabridged.
In other aspects, this book may
vary from the original edition.
Printed in the United States of America
on permanent paper.
Set in 16-point Times New Roman type.

ISBN: 978-1-61173-515-4

Library of Congress Cataloging-in-Publication Data

Macomber, Debbie.
Love thy neighbor : a vintage Debbie Macomber novel / Debbie
Macomber. — Large print ed.
p. cm. — (Center Point large print edition)
ISBN 978-1-61173-515-4 (library binding : alk. paper)
1. Large type books. I. Title.
PS3563.A2364L68 2012
813′.54—dc23
                                                    2012009858

LOVE THY NEIGHBOR

Fall 2012

Dear Friends,

Welcome to another VINTAGE Debbie Macomber story. I wrote LOVE THY NEIGHBOR on a rented typewriter I set up on my kitchen table back in the early 1980's. Technology has certainly changed since then, hasn't it? It's hard to remember what our lives were like before cell phones, personal PC's and the Internet. I have a friend whose grandmother crossed the prairie as an infant in a covered wagon and before she died in the 1960's, she flew on a jet plane. Amazing, isn't it?

Yet it doesn't matter when a book is written; a good story remains a good story. I believe you'll enjoy *Love Thy Neighbor* despite the fact no one has a cell phone or a computer. In addition, significant changes have taken place in the attitudes toward working women. Think of it as a time capsule: a look back to the way things were back then . . . once upon a time.

These days, I am connected on just about every bit of social media available. You can reach me at my website www.DebbieMacomber.com or on Facebook. You can even download a Debbie Macomber app for your cell phone! And as always, you can reach me via snail mail at P.O. Box 1458, Port Orchard, WA 98366. Choose any option . . . I do so enjoy hearing from my readers.

So please, look beyond the obvious changes the years have made and simply enjoy this story.

Warmest regards,

Debbie Macomber

To Les Carr,
the best chauffeur
a teenage girl ever had.

Chapter One

Lesley Brown watched as her newest employee struggled to maintain her poise. Fifty-year-old Charlotte Lewis had been hired at Statewide Savings Bank last month and had proved herself capable of dealing with every aspect of banking. But today was her first day handling new accounts. The older woman looked red-faced and flustered. Frustration drove deep grooves into her smooth brow as she cast Lesley a pleading glance.

Lesley's natural reaction was to respond to Charlotte's silent plea, but that wouldn't help either of them. Every employee was left to deal with an impatient customer occasionally. Like everyone else, Charlotte would need to learn to react courteously and politely. Lesley realized this could sometimes be difficult, but she prided herself on the ability to keep a cool head and a calming demeanor.

Centering her attention on the loan application on her desk, Lesley ignored the raised voices from the other side of the room. With experienced skill, she ran down the printed form, checking to see that all the information had been completed.

"I'm sorry to bother you." Charlotte stood at Lesley's desk, her hands clenched tightly at her sides. "But Mr. Daniels has asked to speak to the manager."

"What seems to be the problem?"

"Actually, there are several. Mr. Daniels has recently moved into the area and wishes to open an account with a check issued from Indiana. I explained the bank's policy regarding checks issued from out of state, but he insists upon talking to someone in authority."

"I understand, Charlotte. Don't worry, you did the right thing." Lesley rolled back her chair and stood. Her high heels tapped against the tile floor as she moved across the room.

"Mr. Daniels." She extended her hand and introduced herself. "I'm Lesley Brown. Is there something I can do for you?"

His handshake was short and barely civil. "I said I wanted to speak to the manager." The dark eyes became narrowed slits. His gaze swept from the top of her dark chestnut-colored, shoulder-length hair down the full extent of her five-foot-five frame. Apparently what he saw didn't please him. One side of his mouth lifted mockingly.

"Mr. Fullbright is out of the office. I'm the assistant manager."

"I'll wait for Mr. Fullbright," he stated dismissively, and glanced at his watch.

"Mr. Daniels, I'm sure I can settle any problem."

Again the dark eyes ran over her. Boldly she met his glare. He was tall and lean, his jaw angular and sharp. But his eyes were what drew her attention. Dark and ruthless, they seemed to possess the sharpness of a hawk's. Lesley doubted that much escaped his notice. If it hadn't been for the contempt in his eyes and the tightly reined impatience about him, she might have thought him attractive. She noted he wasn't wearing a wedding ring. He looked like the urbane type who would prefer to play the field than settle for one woman. Definitely not a man who would interest her.

As if aware of her censure, his mouth formed into an unyielding, hard line, his displeasure stamped on every feature.

So be it, Lesley mused. She didn't particularly care for the way he was arrogantly appraising her either.

"Mr. Daniels would like to open a checking account with an out-of-state check," Charlotte inserted, handing Lesley the check.

"I'm sure Mrs. Lewis explained that we must allot ten days for this to clear before issuing you checks for your account." The question was directed to him.

"She's explained that several times," he returned with marked patience, his tone sarcastic and dry. "But if you'd simply place a phone call, you'd be assured that the check is good."

"I'm sorry, Mr. Daniels, but that's not the way things are done. Coeur d'Alene isn't a vast metropolis; we move cautiously here. The check must—"

"When will the manager be back?" he interrupted her angrily.

"Mr. Daniels." Lesley could feel her own impatience rising. "Let me assure you Mr. Fullbright will say the same thing."

One corner of his mouth edged up in cynical amusement. "Now, that's something I doubt. What a woman's doing in a job that demands common sense and cool-headed reasoning is beyond me. You should be smiling sweetly from behind the counter. A woman has no place in bank management."

"I assure you I am perfectly qualified for my job." Lesley could feel her calm façade evaporating with every sharp word.

"Why don't you go total up figures and leave the real business of running a bank to those who can properly handle it," he declared in cutting tones that aroused the attention of customers, who turned to stare openly at the small group.

"I can see that it isn't going to do any good to explain the bank's point of view. If you prefer to speak with Mr. Fullbright, then you're encouraged to do so. Now, if you'll excuse me." Seething, she pivoted and stalked back to her desk.

Boorish, chauvinist, ill-mannered beast. Her fingers were shaking as she sat down and picked up her pencil. That man had a chip on his shoulder so big it made a California redwood look like an acorn.

The indignation persisted when Lesley pulled into her driveway that night. Her confrontation with Daniels had weighed heavily on her most of the day, and she sat quietly in the car an extra minute, enjoying the unexpected warmth of an Indian summer afternoon.

As Lesley slipped out of the driver's seat, she noted a sports car parked in the driveway on the other side of the duplex. She couldn't identify the make, but it looked fancy and expensive. Apparently the place had been rented. Swinging the long strap of her leather purse over her shoulder, Lesley wondered how long it would be before she met her new neighbor.

The duplex was in a quiet section of town, her nearest neighbors half a block away. Lesley didn't even bother to lock her front door. What did she have that anyone would want? Besides, if someone was determined to steal her things, they could rip out the door lock. In some ways her view of life could be looked upon as dangerously simplistic. But this was a small Idaho town, and she knew and trusted everyone.

At least once she was home she could remove the ambitious businesswoman façade and be herself. Changing into jeans and a red-checked, short-sleeved blouse, she slid open the back door to inspect her garden. Large tomatoes weighted the vines. Many of the green ones wouldn't have time to ripen before the first frost, and she picked several to take inside. The zucchini were still abundant, and she bent down to retrieve one. The pumpkin was large and turning orange. Dinner tonight would consist of a fresh vegetable salad, cheese and leftover roast.

She placed the vegetables in the sink and poured herself a glass of iced tea. Amid the loveliness of the afternoon, the world seemed filled with good things. The grass felt cool and welcoming as she sat, crossed her knees and leaned back to rest her weight on the palms of her hands. She chewed on a long blade of grass and tried to guess what kind of neighbor God had sent her.

Not that anyone could replace her sister, brother-in-law and niece. She was going to miss Terry, Robert and baby Lisa. The little family had become a big part of her life over the past year. Times like now, when she would normally have shared the tea with her sister, made it seem as if Terry was across the world instead of across town. But they had quickly outgrown the one-bedroom duplex after Lisa was born. It was so convenient living next door to one another that Terry had delayed the move for as long as possible. With mixed feelings, Lesley had helped her sister look for a house. They had hugged each other and cried when the last box had been loaded onto the rented moving van and the time had finally arrived for Terry and Robert to drive away.

But before Terry had climbed into the van, the two sisters had walked around the vacant apartment. Together they had prayed for whomever God would move into the duplex. The words of the prayer returned to Lesley now as she stared at the closed sliding glass door of her neighbor's apartment. Terry had promised to continue praying for Lesley's new neighbor. They prayed that whoever the Lord sent to the second half of the duplex would be someone special in her life. Now, alone on the grass, Lesley echoed that prayer.

Whoever had moved in would soon realize that the walls were paper-thin. Terry and Lesley often had to laugh because it was apparent, just from the sounds echoing through, what the other was doing. Countless times they had borrowed things from each other, shared the clothesline and weeded the communal garden. Water pressure had been a problem, but they'd learned to coordinate usage. Lesley would consider herself lucky to find someone as compatible as her sister.

The glass door that opened into the common backyard was closed, the drapes pulled. Lesley wondered who would want to keep the sun out on such a glorious afternoon. But whoever it was, Lesley felt God had specifically sent that family or person. Hadn't she and Terry prayed for just that?

The radio was playing softly in the background as she ripped the lettuce leaves apart for her salad. On an impulse, she pulled out an extra bowl and made two huge salads: one for her, one for her new neighbor. She would take it over as a way of introducing herself.

Adding a dab of gloss to her full mouth, she did a quick inspection in the bathroom mirror. No one was going to call a Hollywood producer, but she looked presentable.

She pushed in the doorbell and listened to the buzz.

Nothing.

Lesley rang the bell again. The fancy sports car was still in the driveway, but that didn't necessarily mean there was someone inside the house. She was about to return to her apartment when the door was jerked open.

In retrospect, Lesley didn't know who looked more shocked, Daniels or herself.

"You!" she gasped, her mouth dropping open.

"Well, if it isn't Little Miss Bank Executive." His voice was low and filled with mocking amusement. "Have you come to apologize and request my business?"

"Oh, hardly." She jerked the salad behind her back. Lettuce leaves fell onto the concrete step.

Purposefully she had returned to her duties that afternoon, forcing herself to concentrate on her work. Lesley had been unaware of how long, if at all, Daniels had waited for Ben Fullbright. "I'm here because . . ." She searched frantically for a plausible excuse. There had been some horrible, dreadful mistake. God wouldn't send someone like Daniels to be her neighbor.

"Yes?" He sounded bored and irritable.

"I'm your neighbor," she managed finally.

He started to laugh then—not a friendly, amused laugh, but one filled with irony, brittle with sarcasm.

Lesley could feel the hairs at the back of her neck bristle. Never had she felt such intense dislike for anyone. One demeaning glance from him assured her that the feeling was mutual. It took more restraint then she wanted to admit not to dump the bowl of salad greens over his head.

"What did you want?" he demanded, his gaze cutting into her.

"Want?" She stared at him blankly.

"You rang *my* doorbell."

He made it sound as if she'd tossed eggs at his windows.

"Yes, I did," she returned awkwardly. "I brought

you dinner as a . . ." The word "welcome" wouldn't make it past the tight knot in her throat.

If possible, the dark eyes hardened all the more. "Let's get one thing straight right now. I don't want to be neighborly. You leave me alone and I'll leave you alone. You stay on your half and I'll stay on mine. Understood?"

"Oh, I understand all right—and concur. I wouldn't want to have anything to do with you if I were stuck in quicksand and couldn't reach a branch." Immediately Lesley recognized how silly she sounded. Under any other circumstances she would have burst out laughing, but there was nothing amusing about Daniels. Nothing!

She stalked across the yard and slammed her front door. Furious, she paced the small enclosure like a trapped panther. Not in twenty-three years had she met anyone she disliked more. He was awful, the epitome of everything she loathed.

Hands hugging her stomach, she paused in the middle of the living room floor, her foot tapping irritably against the worn carpet. A mistake had been made. Something wasn't right. God wouldn't present that bitter, hard, unreasonable man next door on purpose. All she had to do was stay calm and wait for him to leave. And that was exactly what she would do until God rectified the error.

Daniels' fancy sports car was gone the next morning when Lesley left for the bank. With *him* living so close, she decided her things were in imminent danger and locked the front door.

By the time she pulled into her usual parking space on the side street opposite the bank, she was feeling ridiculous. Daniels wasn't going to rob her. True, he was an unpleasant fellow, but they could learn to live in harmony. All she had to do was pretend the apartment was still vacant. That would be easy enough. He would probably be gone by the end of the month, anyway.

Lesley had been at her desk only a matter of minutes when Daniels strolled in. Instinctively she stiffened. Without being obvious, she followed his movements. First he went to a teller who smiled provocatively, obviously taken in by his charm. What charm, Lesley's mind tossed back instantly. The young teller pointed to Ben Fullbright's desk.

With even-paced strides, Daniels walked up to the bank manager's desk and introduced himself. Ben rose and they shook hands.

"Lesley, call on line one," Charlotte Lewis said from the desk beside hers. "Lesley," she repeated.

Lesley jerked upright. "Oh, sorry, what did you say?"

Charlotte repeated the information and Lesley reached automatically for the phone. It was a local resident requesting loan information, and Lesley was tied up for several minutes answering questions.

When she replaced the receiver, Lesley noted

that Ben Fullbright was standing behind the counter for new accounts and was completing the necessary information for Daniels.

The two men shook hands, then Daniels strode toward her desk. Lesley pretended an inordinate interest in the blank form. Although he stood directly in front of her, Lesley didn't glance up, hoping that Daniels would take the hint and leave.

"Miss Brown."

With exaggerated care, Lesley lifted her gaze. "Yes?" Her voice was barely civil.

"I thought you'd like to see these." He laid twenty-five freshly issued blank checks on her desk and riffled them with his thumb.

Closing her eyes and inhaling a deep breath enabled Lesley to hold her temper. "Statewide Savings does its best to keep every customer satisfied. I'm pleased we could be of service," she managed in a starched tone.

"Except that it took a man to listen to reason. I suggest you leave the decision making where it belongs."

"And I suggest you leave me alone before I throw this cup of coffee in your face," she informed him with a wide smile that conveyed the fact she wasn't kidding.

Challenge, mockery, and amusement all glittered from his dark eyes as he dipped his head in acknowledgment. "Good day, Miss Brown." A smile tugged at the corner of his mouth.

"Good day." Purposely she lowered her eyes to her desk. Her heart hammered wildly and her breath came in uneven gulps. Never had she disliked anyone so intensely. Lesley fumed with anger until she heard him turn and walk away.

During her lunch hour, Lesley had a date with Dale Wylie, a new-car salesman, at a local café for lunch.

"Hi, honey, how are things going?" He kissed her lightly on the cheek and slid into the booth, opposite Lesley.

Lesley's gaze followed Dale. "I wish you wouldn't do that."

Dale looked up from the menu with that innocent look she detested. "Do what?"

"Come in here and act like we're an old married couple," she told him forcefully. "We're friends, nothing more. I don't like you giving people the impression there's something more between us."

Dale laid the menu aside. Half the single women in Coeur d'Alene would give anything to have the urbane and good-looking Dale interested in them. Why he'd picked her, Lesley didn't know. They weren't the least alike, didn't share the same interests and often disagreed, especially about Lesley's strong religious convictions. Maybe he thought of her as a challenge. She'd given up trying to guess.

"My, my, you must have had a difficult

morning." His blue eyes shone with sympathy. "Want to tell me about it?"

"I had a wonderful morning, thank you." She hid her expressive eyes behind the menu. She wasn't going to fool Dale, but talking about Daniels wouldn't do any good, either.

Gratefully, he didn't pursue the subject. Lesley doubted that he would: Dale's interest revolved around Dale.

"You'll be pleased to know I made a sale this morning."

"Congratulations. Anyone I know?" She laid the menu aside, genuinely interested.

"I don't think so. New fellow in town, Cole Daniels."

Cole Daniels! Lesley's hand tightened around the water glass.

"Interesting fellow, seemed to know a lot about cars. Paid cash."

She nodded, hoping he wouldn't notice the way she'd stiffened when he rolled off the name. So Daniels' first name was Cole. It should have been *Cold*.

"I know him," she said lightly, twisting the spoon with her fingers in nervous reaction. "Did he trade in that fancy sports car of his?"

"Sports car? No, he didn't, he walked into the showroom. He didn't have any wheels." Dale's mouth quirked briefly. "How do you know him?"

"He moved into the other half of the duplex."

24

Dale's look narrowed and he regarded her seriously. "I'm not sure I approve of the two of you living next to each other like that."

"What?" Lesley swallowed a gasp of resentment.

"Separated from the rest of the town like that," he hurried to explain.

"I'll tell you what," she began, deliberately setting the spoon aside and raising her eyes to his, "if you can figure a way to get him out of there, I wouldn't object."

"You wouldn't?"

"Not in the least. I find the man to be opinionated and irksome. Terry and I were such good friends, but I can't imagine Cole Daniels and me ever getting along."

"Well, in that case, I can't see much of a problem."

Men! Lesley felt like screaming. All they ever cared about was themselves. How could her sister be married and so happy?

"I'm not very hungry, Dale. If you don't mind, I think I'll skip lunch today." She started to slide out of the booth.

"I knew there was something wrong." Dale sounded pleased with himself for such keen insight. "You're not feeling well, are you? Headache?"

Her confirming nod wasn't a lie. Every minute she spent in Dale's company only made her head pound worse.

"Before you go." A hand on her forearm stopped her. "We'd better decide what we're wearing to Larry's party."

Could the day get any worse? "Larry's party?" she echoed. Maybe if she played dumb they could avoid another confrontation.

"The Halloween bash next weekend. I already told him we were coming."

"You did what?" she asked, her eyes spitting fire.

"Now, hold on, there's no need to get all upset." He patted her arm soothingly as if she were a recalcitrant child.

"I told you," she said in measured tones, "I have no intention of attending that party. I'm going to the one at the church. I thought I made that extremely clear."

"Let me explain before you become unreasonable," Dale returned calmly. "I'm not insensitive, I know this thing at your church is important to you. I want you to go, but there's no reason you can't attend both. You can give me a call and I'll swing by the church to pick you up. As I see it, you won't even need to change costumes."

"Everyone's dressing up as Bible characters. Can't you see how ludicrous it would be to go from church to Larry's?"

"Not necessarily," Dale inserted. "Who are you going as?"

"Lot's wife."

"Lot's wife? But she—"

"I know," Lesley interrupted. "I'm dressing up as a pillar of salt."

Amusement gleamed briefly from his eyes. "That sounds like a good idea, but you probably should wear something that will fit in at both parties."

"Dale." Lesley slid out of the booth, and took a step in backward retreat. "Read my lips, because I have the feeling you never hear what I'm saying," she instructed. "I'm not going to Larry's party. Not this year, not ever. You know what I think of Larry O'Brien; I don't want to have anything to do with him."

"Lesley"—Dale murmured her name softly—"I'm sure you don't mean that."

What more did she have to say to reach this man? "I mean it, Dale." Rather than argue further, she turned sharply and left the café.

The afternoon was another glorious one, but Lesley hardly noticed. What was the matter with her lately? Everything was going wrong.

Instead of going straight back to the bank, she strolled down the street, stopping in a couple of shops along the way to browse.

"He was so handsome. Mark my words, that man has broken a few hearts in his day."

Lesley picked up part of a conversation between a cashier and a housewife. Her interest sparked, Lesley stood behind a counter pretend-

27

ing to examine a sweater as she listened to the conversation.

"Said his name was Cole Daniels."

Hot color invaded her face. Was her ill-mannered neighbor going to haunt her all day?

"Tight-lipped, though," the woman continued. "Hardly said a word. Just paid for his purchase. I asked if he was from around here, and he said he wasn't."

"Did you ask where he's from?"

Lesley was more than interested and silently berated herself for eavesdropping so blatantly. She hadn't done anything like this since Terry was sixteen and standing on the porch talking to her dates.

"I asked, but he didn't say."

The check he'd deposited had been issued from Indiana; Lesley knew that much.

"He didn't seem inclined to talk about himself. Probably just passing through."

"Probably," the other woman agreed.

Silently, Lesley hoped they were both right.

The remainder of the afternoon proved to be uneventful. At five o'clock Lesley walked out of the building with Ben Fullbright. He, at least, didn't mention Cole Daniels, and Lesley was more than grateful.

"See you in the morning." She gave Ben a small wave, waited at the crosswalk, then ran across the busy street to her parked car.

The car's interior felt warm and stuffy, unusual for late October. Lesley scooted inside and immediately rolled down the window. A cooling breeze flowed through the vehicle, whipping her hair across her face as she headed for home.

Her first impulse was to drive over to Terry's. She'd spent several days helping her sister unpack and settle in the new house. But Lesley hesitated. When Terry lived next door there was always an excuse to see each other, do something together. Things were different now, and should be. Terry, Robert and the baby were a family in themselves. And although it felt awkward not to share some of the things that had been happening with Terry, Lesley recognized it was for the best.

Since she'd skipped lunch, Lesley was hungry and pulled into a little mom-and-pop grocery store. The Walkers couldn't hope to compete with the large supermarkets, but their service was always friendly and warm. Both Paul and Martha Walker were strong Christian people, and Lesley liked to give them as much business as she could afford.

Absently she noted that there was only one other car parked in front of the store. She pushed open the glass door and smiled brightly. Her mouth froze. Cole Daniels was standing in front of the outdated cash register. Groceries lined the counter.

"Afternoon, Lesley." Paul Walker glanced up, a look of distinct relief touching his eyes. "Guess you could say it was providential you stopping in today."

"Oh?" Her hand clenched the strap of her purse tightly.

"Mr. Daniels is here, and being new to the community and all . . ." Paul hesitated.

"What he really wants to know is if the check is good."

"You being from the bank . . ." Walker added.

The challenge in Cole Daniels' eyes was unmistakable. He stood tall and proud, almost daring Lesley to deny that he had enough money in his account to pay for his goods.

Self-consciously Lesley glanced from one man to the other. "Mr. Daniels opened his account with us today with a generous amount. I'm sure his check is fine."

Relief eased the age lines from the old man's weathered face. "No offense intended, but I can't stand to take a loss for this amount."

"I understand," Cole Daniels returned in a surprisingly sympathetic voice.

Cole left the market before Lesley. She made an excuse to linger, not wanting to see him again if she could avoid it, staying in the back of the store until she heard him leave.

After carefully inspecting the meat available in the small cooler, Lesley purchased a cube steak, julienned green beans and lettuce for a salad. She nibbled on a package of potato chips as she laid the few items on the counter.

"Seems like a nice fellow," Mr. Walker began.

"Who?" She was being deliberately obtuse. Cole Daniels had been invading her safe, secure world all day. She couldn't take much more of the irritating stranger.

"Daniels," Paul Walker said and gave her a funny look. "I hated to ask about the check, but he didn't have his name or address printed on it."

"I'm sure he will later." Lesley strove to sound nonchalant.

"I told him if he was going to buy that many groceries, it would be cheaper for him to go to a supermarket. I can't compete with their prices." His hands busily rang up her purchases on the antique cash register, then bagged her few items into a brown paper sack. "I didn't want to lose his business, but I hated to see him waste good money."

Paul Walker had to be the most unselfish Christian man she had ever known, Lesley decided. How many others who were working to keep a business going would have made such a suggestion?

"We don't get many strangers this time of year," he added.

Lesley agreed with a quick nod. "I know."

"How long is he staying?"

31

She motioned weakly with her hands. "He didn't say, but since he's rented the duplex and opened a checking account, I'd say he intends to be here awhile."

"Don't suppose you know what line of work he's in?"

"Not a clue." She paid for her things and lifted the grocery sack off the counter. "Wish I could be more help, but I don't know much of anything."

Paul Walker placed the money in the till. "I don't mean to be such a gossip."

The Walkers were nothing of the sort. "I'm sure you didn't," she assured him.

"Don't know what it is about the man." He paused to rub his chin with a thumb. "Sometimes the Lord gives me certain feelings about people. I took one look at him and could almost see the bitterness."

Lesley had felt that too.

"But more than that, I sensed he was running—not because he's in trouble with the law, but running scared from unhappiness and life."

Lesley noted that, as he spoke, a soft look came over Paul Walker's face. The old man hesitated. "Cole Daniels needs our prayers."

She couldn't agree with him more.

Chapter Two

Lesley carried her small bag of groceries into the house. Cole's new car was parked in his driveway. What had happened to the flashy sports car she saw yesterday? Had he parked it in the garage? She'd only seen it that one time. And although she wasn't much of an auto expert, she knew enough to realize it was no ordinary vehicle.

The house felt unusually warm and stuffy. Leaving the grocery sack on the kitchen counter, Lesley immediately opened the sliding glass door. She stood in the open doorway and unfastened the top button of her crisp linen business suit. Appreciatively, she paused to inhale the fresh, country-scented air. Slipping off her pumps, she flexed her toes and pulled her silk blouse free from her waistband. In a matter of minutes the transformation from rising bank executive to down-home country girl—complete with jeans—was complete.

Whistling, she cut the steak into thin strips, added a few vegetables and broth and left it to simmer.

The garden fork was set against the back of the house. With the weather so unusually warm, it would be a good time to till under a portion of the garden. The work was strenuous, and she stopped several times to wipe the perspiration from her brow. Once she felt as if someone was watching her, but when she turned around, no one was there.

Rubbing the palms of her hands on the back pockets of her jeans, she stuck the fork in the ground and walked over to the side of the house to get the hose.

She could hear that Cole was running water. With a satisfied smirk she planned her small revenge. It seemed Cole Daniels was about to receive his first lesson in the problems the duplex had with water pressure. With a smile tugging at the corners of her mouth, she turned the faucet as far as it would go. Nothing happened at first, but soon an even flow of water ran from the tap.

She dragged the hose to the area she'd recently tilled and sprayed water over the grass and leaves she'd laid on top of the earth. Not more than two minutes later, Cole stormed out the back door.

"Just what do you think you're doing?" he demanded.

Startled, Lesley dropped the nozzle and swung around. "What do you mean?" she yelled back. If he hadn't been so angry, she would have laughed. Cole was dressed in jeans, his feet bare.

His shirt was left open and clung to his wet torso. His damp hair was standing straight on end as if someone had electrocuted him.

Hands on hips, she met his furious glare. "Is there a problem?"

"You're darn right there is. I was in the shower when the water suddenly turned into a cold trickle."

"You can't blame me for that."

"Just whose fault is it, then?"

"The city, the landlord and in some ways the state of Idaho."

"Don't get cute with me, little girl."

"Little girl?" she fumed. "Well, listen up, bub, how was I supposed to know you were in the shower?"

"You mean to tell me I have to report to you every time I flush the toilet?"

"Now, that's just a mite different from washing clothes or taking a shower. We're going to have to work out a time schedule."

"No way."

"Fine with me." Ignoring him as best she could, Lesley swung around, picked up the hose and continued to douse the garden."

"Turn that off!" he shouted.

"No way," she returned in his own words.

Hands clenched at his sides, Cole raged across the yard, heading for the outside faucet.

"I'd advise you to stay away from that," Lesley

shouted, "or you'll be getting a lot more than a cold trickle." She jiggled the hose a couple of times to prove she wasn't fooling.

"Threats, Lesley?" His voice was low and dangerous.

Goose bumps broke out across her forearms at the chill in his voice. "I'm warning you," she said with much bravado.

"Yes?" He took a step closer.

"Don't." She retreated, her resolve wavering. What was the matter with her? Show some mettle, her mind shouted. Straightening her shoulders, she faced him boldly. "We could compromise," she suggested, angry with herself for the way her voice wobbled. She wasn't some country hick he could push around.

"The solution is simple."

"Oh?"

"Turn off that thing, I'll finish my shower and then you can do as you please."

In a burst of temper, Lesley threw down the green garden hose, stalked to the faucet and turned off the water. Hands placed challengingly on hips, she whirled around. "There. Are you happy?"

He made an indifferent sound as if what she did or didn't do wasn't of interest to him, and the irritating way he looked and spoke only served to fuel the temper stirring within her. Was she safe with this kind of man living next door? Paul

Walker had sensed that things weren't right with Cole Daniels, confirming her own feelings.

"Before you go in, I think there's something you should know," Lesley warned.

"Yes?"

Lesley assumed the defensive stance her instructor had shown her. Her hands were positioned level with her face. Baring her teeth for effect, she glared at him. "I've had four karate lessons."

His robust laugh only angered her more. The man was despicable. She felt ridiculously close to tears and fluttered her lashes furiously at the smarting moistness. She never cried.

"Is that supposed to frighten me?" Cole asked.

"No!" she shouted, afraid the brightness of unshed tears might shine from her eyes. "But . . . I think you should know I can take care of myself."

The humor drained from his eyes. His entire demeanor changed, and Lesley couldn't understand why. A hard mask seemed to steal over his face. "Good. Finish those lessons. You may need them."

Lesley paused long enough to grab her purse and sweater and lock the front door. Then she drove straight to her sister's.

"Terry!" She burst in the front door, her voice urgent and confused.

Terry rushed out of the kitchen, the wooden door swinging after her. "What is it?"

"A man moved in next door."

Immediately Terry's expression relaxed. "Oh dear. For a minute you had me frightened. A man, you say. How interesting. Married?"

"I don't know." Her sister apparently didn't understand the situation, and from the look in her eye, the romantic side of Terry's nature had taken over. Lesley could almost see the little wheels in her sister's mind whirling a hundred miles an hour.

"Is he wearing a wedding band?"

"No." She swallowed a giant breath. "It's not what you think."

"He's old."

"No."

"Good. Young and handsome?"

"You could say that. Terry! Stop and listen to me."

"I'm listening," she returned with a distant look in her eye.

Only a year separated the two sisters, and when they dressed alike, it was difficult to tell them apart. Both had the rich chestnut-colored hair and sky-blue eyes that altered to a vibrant gray when they were excited or angry. High cheekbones and rosy complexion were a family trademark.

"I'm home." Robert announced and the back screen door slammed, hailing his entry.

Terry kissed her husband and wrapped an arm

around his waist. "Lesley's new neighbor is a man."

"Interesting." Robert replied after he'd nuzzled Terry's neck.

"No it's not," Lesley insisted. "I wish the two of you would listen to me. He's awful. Despicable."

"Unreasonable?" Terry added.

"Yes." Some of the apprehension drained out of her. Maybe Terry did understand.

"They're the best kind," Terry said knowingly. The baby let out a loud cry from the back bedroom. "Lisa's awake. Will you get her for me?"

Although she dearly loved her niece, Lesley didn't think Lisa could have picked a worse time to wake up from her nap.

"What's for dinner?"

Lesley heard Robert's question as she moved down the narrow hall to the bedroom portion of the house. What was the matter with everyone today? A strange man had moved in next to her, and Terry acted as if she'd been told Lesley had won the Irish Sweepstakes.

Eighteen-month-old Lisa was standing, her tiny hands clenching the crib bars. When she saw Lesley, she gurgled happily.

"Hello, Lisa," Lesley said in the singsong voice the child loved. "How's Auntie Lesley's little girl?"

Lisa held up both hands, wanting to be taken

out of the crib. Lesley lifted the baby into her arms, changed her diaper and carried her back into the living room.

Robert was reading the newspaper, his stocking feet propped against the coffee table. Lisa gave a cry of delight, and Lesley placed the little girl on the floor and watched as the baby ran to her father's arms. Robert scooted Lisa onto his lap. Together the two sat contentedly and read the paper.

Terry was in the kitchen frying hamburger. "Can't you see I'm upset?" Lesley said in an accusing tone.

"About your new neighbor?" Terry opened the refrigerator and took out a block of Cheddar cheese. "I don't understand why. We prayed, didn't we?"

"Then God made a mistake."

Terry laughed. "Think about what you just said."

"I have. God would never move someone as horrible as Cole Daniels next to me. Obviously whoever is supposed to be there got held up for some reason and this fellow will be moving on."

"Then there's no reason to worry, is there?"

Leave it to Terry to remain calm and sensible. "Yes there is."

"Why?"

Lesley gestured defeatedly with her hand. "I'm not sure. But things aren't what they should be with this guy. He's so unfriendly, almost secretive. It's hard to explain."

"And you've got a creative imagination."

"I knew you were going to say that," Lesley cried. "I suppose you're going to bring up the time I thought someone was kidnapping Mom."

"The thought entered my mind." Terry sliced off a piece of cheese and handed it to Lesley. "This is a new smoked flavor; what do you think?"

"It's good," Lesley murmured absently. "Terry, *please* would you take me seriously."

Terry looked up surprised. "I am."

"You're not," her sister accused.

"What would you like me to do?"

"I don't know. But something. I . . . I don't trust this guy."

"Then lock your door."

"I have."

Lesley leaned against the counter, crossing her feet at the ankle. She hung her head, thinking over how much of the conversation with Cole she wanted to relate to her sister. The memory of her actions made her realize how ridiculous the whole thing had been.

"Maybe I should be more concerned." Terry broke into her thoughts, and her eyes flickered over her sister briefly. "But I've continued to pray about this neighbor thing."

"You have?" Lesley's head shot up.

41

"If you want to know the truth, I've been worried about you lately."

"Me?"

Terry stretched a piece of plastic wrap across the top of the cheese. Her gaze avoided Lesley's. "I know how you feel about Dale and I know"—she took in a deep breath and hesitated—"that you're not seeing anyone else. So I started praying that God would bring a new man into your life."

"You're nuts! Do you mean to tell me that you've been praying that God would move a man in next door?" Gathering speed, her words seemed to stumble over her tongue. "And . . . and not just any man, mind you, but an unreasonable, mysterious, boorish chauvinist?"

Lesley witnessed the silent laugh her sister struggled to disguise as Terry turned and pretended to stir the already cooked meat. "Nothing so dramatic," she said at last.

"What, then?"

"Well, I've continued to pray about the neighbor situation, that's true, but I assumed another girl would move in." She hooked a long strand of dark hair around her ear. "I don't know why. But I have been wondering about you and Dale."

"I don't want to talk about him."

Terry set the spoon on a dish at the side of the stove and turned. "Are you two fighting again?"

"I said I didn't want to talk about it."

Linking her hands behind her back, Terry shrugged. "See what I mean?"

Not willing to admit anything, but unable to ignore the taut line of her sister's mouth or the concern etched about her eyes, Lesley nodded.

"You need someone new in your life." Terry's voice was gentle, loving. "That's been my prayer. You can't be angry with me for that, can you?"

Dusk was purpling the sky when Lesley pulled into her driveway and shut off the car's engine. The conversation with her sister had been more disconcerting than she cared to admit. Her thoughts remained troubled as she opened the door. The aroma of stewing meat captured her immediate attention.

What was the matter with her appetite? No lunch and no interest in dinner.

The phone rang, jerking her attention beyond the kitchen.

"Hello."

"It's about time you got home. Just where have you been?"

"Evening, Dale." Lesley released a slow breath and ignored his question. "What can I do for you?"

"The party. I want you to know you're going to Larry's party with me or that's it. In other words, we're finished, through, over."

The decision wasn't even difficult. "Then so be it," she told him stiffly.

"Listen, baby, you don't mean that." Dale's tone grew coaxing and gentle. "What's the matter with a little fun now and then?" The sound of his laughter was slurred.

So Dale had been drinking again. He was probably with Larry. She couldn't see fighting with him, especially over the phone. "We'll talk about it tomorrow."

"Meet me for lunch?"

"Okay." Reluctantly Lesley agreed. She didn't want to be subjected to another confrontation of wills. No matter how adamant she felt about Larry's party, Dale dismissed her feelings. Terry was right. This mixed-up relationship with Dale must end, and the sooner the better.

With growing concern over the craziness her life seemed to have taken on over the past couple of weeks, Lesley forced herself to eat dinner.

After doing the dishes, she set up the sewing machine on the kitchen table and brought out the white material she'd purchased for the church Halloween costume. The radio was playing mellow sounds, and soon Lesley found herself involved in the project, her troubles forgotten as she sang and worked.

A loud knock on the front door froze her actions. Removing the straight pins from her mouth, she hesitated long enough to murmur an

44

urgent prayer that her visitor wasn't Dale. Several times in the past he'd phoned her when he'd been drinking, but she'd never had to deal with him physically.

The doorbell chimed in short, impatient rings. Clenching and unclenching her fist, Lesley looked out the front window. Dale's car wasn't in her driveway. But unfortunately she couldn't see who was on her step. With no choice, she opened the door.

Cole Daniels glared at her irritably. "For someone who can take care of herself with her vast and intimate knowledge of karate, it took you long enough to answer the door."

Lesley decided to disregard his sarcasm rather than argue with him.

"What do you want?" she asked pointedly.

"What are the walls made of, anyway? Cardboard?"

"Are you trying to tell me the radio's too loud?" How could anyone object to the soothing sounds of mellow music?

"The radio's fine. I'll listen to that. It's you I can't take."

"Me?" She folded her arms across her chest in a pure instinctively protective habit. It was either that or slam the door in his face. What was there about this one man that could make her more unreasonable than any other? "Was that all?" Her voice was dipped in acid.

"Please." He pivoted and walked away.

Lesley closed the door and spun around. Her sister had been praying that God would send a man into her life? That ill-mannered beast couldn't possibly be him. She didn't need to be a devoted Christian to recognize that a mistake had been made.

Lesley lay awake for a long time that night, her heart heavy. She tried reading the Bible. A smile flickered over her lips. Terry had once told her that if she had trouble sleeping, instead of counting sheep she should talk to the Shepherd.

She liked to think of herself as a strong Christian. She'd been raised in a God-fearing home. From the time she could remember, Jesus had been a large part of her life. She had never done anything without first considering her Christian values. Maybe that was the problem—she hadn't really been exposed to certain things in life. But then, did she want to be? Everything seemed so muddled in her own mind.

Just when she felt she could sleep, Lesley rolled over, tugged the blankets to her shoulder and sighed a prayer. A noise interrupted the peaceful solitude. Her eyes shot open. What was it? Sitting up in bed, Lesley strained to hear the soft tapping sounds. A typewriter? Tossing back the covers, she wandered into the living room and then the kitchen. The sounds were more distinct now: definitely the sounds of a typewriter.

Cole Daniels was a writer? Maybe he was only doing a letter. She opened the refrigerator and poured herself a glass of milk. Sitting on the couch in the darkened room, Lesley pulled her long gown over her legs and wrapped her arms around her knees. After an hour of constant tapping sounds, she decided two could play his game.

Shoving her feet into large fuzzy slippers, Lesley jerked her coat off the hanger, opened the front door and stalked across the driveway.

He didn't answer her first polite tap. She waited and, like him, buzzed the doorbell, in short, impatient rings.

"Yes." He nearly took the hinges off the door when he pulled it open.

"I can't sleep with all that racket you're making."

"Racket?" He looked puzzled. "You mean my typing?"

"You've got it."

One corner of his mouth lifted in a movement that could have been considered a half-smile. "I'll try to hold down the voluminous roar."

"I'd appreciate that. Good night, Mr. Daniels," she said in a stiff, polite voice.

"Miss Brown." He closed the door even before she'd turned around.

Lesley had hung up her coat and returned to her bedroom when her doorbell rang a second time that night. Even Dale had the common decency not to come this late.

With a sense of dread, she opened the front door. "Now what?" she demanded.

Cole was leaning lackadaisically against the doorjamb, a pair of earmuffs dangling from his index finger. "I thought these might solve your problem."

Lesley's back went rigid. "And I assure you the only problem I have is you."

He shrugged as if to say the matter was out of his hands. "Then don't blame me if my typing keeps you awake, because I plan to do exactly that every day and every night until . . ." He left the rest of what he was planning to say go unspoken.

"Until what?" she prompted.

"Never mind." His eyes narrowed. "Good night, Miss Brown."

"Mr. Daniels."

Their eyes met and held: his dark, fighting to disguise his amusement; hers bright and angry.

Gently she closed the door and leaned against it, her hands behind her back. Never had she reacted this strongly to a man.

Lunch with Dale didn't go well the next afternoon—not that Lesley had expected it would. In the end she was forced to insist that she wouldn't attend Larry's party with him. Her decision was received with ill grace, but then she'd known from past experience that Dale was a poor loser.

After work, Lesley changed into her jeans with plans to wash her car. Before turning on the water, she decided to play it safe and let Cole know what she was doing.

Lightly she knocked on his door. The new car was parked in the driveway, but she never knew what to expect with him.

"What do you want now?" He threw open the door, and Lesley had to stifle a startled gasp. It didn't look as if he'd gone to bed. He was wearing the same clothes as the night before. A day's growth of beard darkened his face, and his eyes were narrowed and angry.

"I wanted you to know I was planning to wash my car."

He stared back at her blankly.

"The water pressure." Her eyes regarded him thoughtfully. "Are you all right?"

His confirming nod was swift and abrupt.

"Have you been writing night and day?"

He didn't seem to hear her. Instead he slouched against the frame of the door. Even in his condition there was an air of quiet authority about him.

"You must be exhausted." Lesley didn't know why she should care, but she did.

"Just leave me alone," he lashed out, and rubbed a hand across his face.

"Gladly," she returned in a tightly controlled voice. "I was only trying to save you from being stuck in a cold shower. But at this point it may be just what you need."

Something unreadable shot over his expression. Regret? Anger? Lesley didn't know. But when her gaze met his, a funny sensation raced through her: an awareness of him as a man, and not just any man, but a ruggedly virile specimen. The thought shocked her. She didn't want to think of Cole Daniels as a man. This was Terry's fault. She almost regretted having gone to her sister's yesterday. Their conversation had brought up more questions when Lesley had hoped to have some answered.

Lesley noticed that Cole's features had been darkened by the sun. Yesterday, when he'd come raging at her from the shower, she'd seen how deeply tanned he was, but in her anger the fact hadn't fully registered. The handsome features were marred only by the crinkling lines around his eyes.

Why would anyone who loved the outdoors so much choose to lock himself up in an out-of-the-way duplex? Nothing about Cole Daniels seemed to make sense.

Abruptly he turned away and closed the door. Lesley was left to face the nagging silence alone.

The rest of the week passed without incident. Lesley didn't once see Cole. Late at night she could hear the pounding typewriter keys, but she didn't complain about the noise and he didn't grumble about her singing. The unspoken agreement made for a fragile peace.

Halloween night, Lesley dressed in her costume. A large cone-shaped hat rested on top of her head. An empty salt canister hung around her neck, and the long flowing white gown reached the ground.

Lesley carried out a plate of homemade cookies to the car and returned to the house for the canister of lemonade. Munching on a cookie on her way out the door, she paused in mid-step and nearly stumbled off the stair. Cole Daniels was watching her with amused cynicism. His dark eyes surveyed her from head to foot, then back for a second disbelieving look. "My, my, what do we have here?"

"What do you want?" Lesley frowned. She liked it better when they didn't talk to each other. The fuse to her temper was never shorter than when she had to deal with him.

"Nothing," he denied. He was dressed casually in jeans and a sweater. Lesley was forced to admit he looked ruggedly handsome.

He slipped his hands into his pockets and leaned a shoulder against the doorframe.

"However, I'd be interested in knowing what you're up to." A slow smile moved across his mouth. "You look ridiculous."

Her blue eyes were wide and confused as Cole continued to stare at her flushed face with lazy interest.

"You know what your problem is, Cole Daniels?" Cool challenge narrowed her eyes. "You're suffering from a spiritual disease."

"A what?"

"You heard me. A disease. I've tried everything I know to get along with you. I want you to know that I'm praying for you." Without another word she jumped into the car, yanked it into reverse and backed out of the driveway.

Resentment burned through her blood. Even when she was halfway to the church, Cole's affront hadn't cooled. Maybe if she'd been paying closer attention to what she was doing, Lesley decided later, she might have avoided the accident.

A small dog darted into the street, and Lesley swerved to avoid hitting the animal. Her car jumped the curb and tilted headfirst into the ditch.

For a stunned, breathless second she didn't move. It had all happened so quickly. Lesley sat in a world of unreality. This couldn't really have happened—not to her, not on the way to church dressed up as a pillar of salt.

She didn't move for several moments, then gradually stretched her arms. Nothing seemed to be hurt. All she felt was numb.

Opening the car door, she climbed out to assess the damage, which seemed only minimal: a scratched bumper. Surprisingly, no one had rushed to her aid to make sure she was unhurt. But since it was Halloween, most kids were circulating or collecting candy on the more populated blocks.

A car approached in the distance. In the dark, it was impossible to see who it was.

She straightened and gave a small wave, hoping someone would stop and help her out of the ditch.

A horrid suspicion formed in her mind as the car drew closer. Cole Daniels.

He pulled up alongside of her and rolled down his window.

"You all right?"

"Fine. Not a scratch on me." Nervously she laughed off his concern.

Cole tilted his head to one side. "Seems like you've got yourself into a mess here."

"I know." What did he want her to do, beg for his help? She'd rot first.

"I can see that you're probably suffering from . . . what did you say I had? Oh yes." He tipped back his hat with his index finger. "Spiritual disease. That's what you called it."

"B-but—" she stuttered.

"I want you to know I'll be praying for you." With that he rolled up his window and drove away.

Chapter Three

Lesley stared after Cole in shocked disbelief. "I can't believe that man," she muttered incredulously. As his car advanced down the street, Lesley became more scornful. He wouldn't really leave her, would he? All he wanted was the satisfaction of having her beg. But she refused to play his game.

Both arms hugging her waist, she shuffled her feet anxiously. "It's all your fault anyway," she shouted into the empty street after Cole, willingly placing the blame on him.

A couple of minutes passed, and still the street remained deserted. She could be stuck out here all night. Even the few houses in the immediate vicinity didn't have any lights on. The inhabitants were probably gone for the evening, so it wouldn't do any good to trek up and see about using the phone.

Another few moments, and Lesley looked around her helplessly. If Cole happened to drive by again, she'd be more apt to smile sweetly.

"Darn!" She kicked at the radial tire, stubbed

her toe and wanted to cry with frustration. Everything was going wrong. Everything! What was she suppose to do? Walk down Harrison Avenue garbed in a white sheet as a pillar of salt? That would cause quite a stir. She'd be the laughing stock of Coeur d'Alene.

A pair of headlights could be seen shining in the distance. Hope sprang as Lesley straightened and stepped into the middle of the street. When it looked as if the vehicle might turn, Lesley groaned and gave a shout.

"Here. I'm here." She waved her arm high above her head. "Don't leave, please don't leave."

The car seemed to hesitate, then came her way. Lesley heaved a giant sigh. As it approached, she saw that it was a tow truck.

The vehicle pulled up beside her. "Evening, miss, would you be needing help?" An older man was speaking with a soft southern drawl. He sounded like an angel.

"Yes, yes," Lesley cried eagerly. "You don't know how glad I am to see you. I was getting worried—there doesn't seem to be anyone home around here."

The gray-haired man climbed out of the truck's cab, grinning widely. He tipped his hat back with one hand as he surveyed Lesley's vehicle. "This doesn't look like it'll take much."

"Oh, good." Relief washed over her.

"I'll just attach the cable and haul her out. No problem."

"Wonderful," Lesley murmured and stepped aside as he climbed into his truck and backed it up across the road to position it to the best advantage.

On the street again, he regarded Lesley with curious eyes. "You always dress like that?"

"These? No, I'm on my way to church."

"Church," he repeated with a laugh. "On Halloween? You're likely to get mugged on a night like this."

Her good mood rejuvenated, Lesley responded with a light laugh. "I think I'll take my chances. But next year I'm not changing into my costume until I arrive at the church. I had visions of walking into town in this getup. Can you imagine the looks people would have given me?"

"Man said you'd be real eager to see me."

"Man?" Lesley repeated, slow comprehension seeping into her thoughts.

"Yeah, the guy that pulled into the service station. He said he saw someone in trouble but thought it might be some weirdo and that I should be careful. That's why I came up real cautious like."

Cole Daniels, Lesley seethed. Of all the nerve. "I don't suppose this man was driving a new car."

"That's him," the tow truck operator responded

without looking up, his gaze fixed on the rear bumper of her car. "Real knowledgeable about cars, too." He paused and wiped his hands on a greasy rag that hung from the back of his coveralls pocket.

"How do you mean?"

"Had this foreign job in the garage all week. Couldn't for the life of me figure out what was wrong. Then this guy in the new car pulls up while I'm working on it, and listens to the engine running. Next thing I know, he walks over and moves a couple of wires, and bingo, that baby was purring like a well-fed cat."

"Nice of him," Lesley muttered caustically under her breath. Cole had no difficulty lending a stranger a helping hand, but it didn't seem to bother him to leave her helpless on a deserted street with an empty canister of salt hanging around her neck. Her neighbor was a real jewel, and when she saw him next she'd tell him exactly what she thought.

Lesley's little car came out of the ditch without a problem. She wrote a check to the tow truck operator and thanked him again.

Within a couple of minutes they were both on their way. As much as Lesley tried to put the incident with Cole behind her, she couldn't. He had left her like that on purpose. What kind of brute was he?

The church parking lot was full by the time

Lesley arrived, which didn't help cool her indignation. Hurriedly she delivered the cookies and lemonade to the kitchen and was on her way to the recreation hall when she bumped into Terry.

"Where have you been?" Terry asked in an anxious, high-pitched voice. "I was beginning to get worried."

"Don't ask." Lesley responded with a half groan. "It's a long story."

"I love the costume." Lesley's sister took a step back to examine her.

"Thanks. What have I missed?"

"A few games. Bobbing for apples and the treasure hunt. Nothing much." A brooding look came over Terry's face. "Something's wrong. I think you'd better tell me about it."

"Not now," Lesley said with a sigh. "I'm too angry."

"I don't suppose this has something to do with your new neighbor?"

Lesley could feel the color invade her face. She'd never felt such intense dislike for anyone. All her life her parents had taught her to look for the good in every person and situation. But after tonight she could think of nothing to like about Cole Daniels.

"Yes, it's my neighbor," Lesley admitted after a meaningful pause. "I don't like him, Terry. The two of us seem to clash against each other. My life's going to be miserable until he leaves."

"Les?" Terry's blue-gray eyes probed hers. "I don't think I've ever seen you react this strongly to anyone. You've always been tolerant and good-natured."

"That's what I used to think."

A burst of laughter and applause erupted from the hall.

"Come on." Terry glanced away from her. "If we don't get going, we'll miss the whole party. But promise you'll tell me everything later," she coaxed.

"I promise," Lesley agreed reluctantly. She wasn't looking forward to relaying the incident, mainly because she recognized that her role that evening hadn't been entirely innocent. But if she was completely honest with herself, it wasn't the fact that Cole had left her in the street alone, it was his parting words that irritated her. No matter how they felt about each other, if their roles had been reversed she would never have left him.

The recreation hall was alive with young and old alike as they gathered together for the All Saints' Eve costume party. The gaily dressed youngsters had been divided into age groups and were involved in variety of games. A long table in the rear of the hall was full of carved pumpkins. Robert, wearing a badge that designated him as a judge, was closely examining each one. BRIBES ACCEPTED was sketched in large letters on the bottom of his badge.

"Come on, Robert may need a little help deciding."

The two women weaved their way through the large crowd.

"We thought you might like our opinion," Terry said as she slipped an arm around her husband's waist.

"Nope, my mind's set." He was dressed as one of the apostles. A fake beard was glued to his face. A long brown housecoat was cinched at his middle, and he carried a fishing pole.

"Clever outfit," Lesley commented, her bad mood dissipating under the shouts of laughter and the gay mood of the others.

"What about me?" Terry rotated slowly, her eyes smiling.

Lesley had been so caught up with her anger, she hadn't noticed her sister's outfit. Terry wore a long, draping white gown and a blue head scarf that flowed halfway down her back. Bare feet in sandals, she carried a ceramic pitcher.

"Martha from Bethany. Lazarus' sister?"

"Nope." Terry laughed. "I thought for sure you'd know."

Lesley shrugged in defeat. "I give up. Who are you?"

"The Samaritan woman who met Jesus at the well in the Gospel of John."

"You mean the one with five husbands," Lesley teased.

"Five husbands," Robert echoed loudly.

"That's the one." Lesley watched as her sister lifted laughing eyes to her husband. "So you'd better shape up or I'll move on to husband number two."

Lesley smiled, too. Terry and Robert were so much in love that she could almost be envious. It didn't seem fair that her sister should find someone so easily when she attracted men like Dale Wylie. Terry and Robert had met at church camp on Coeur d'Alene Lake their first year of college. Both were serving as counselors for the fourth, fifth and sixth graders for the summer. In the fall, Robert had gone back to Seattle Pacific University in Washington State while Terry attended the local community college. They wrote one another every day, and Terry lived for the holidays when Robert would be back in town. They were married two years later. Why couldn't she have met someone at summer camp? The thought was so ridiculous that it prompted one side of her mouth upward to form a lopsided grin.

". . . And you look ridiculous." Lesley picked up on the second half of Robert's statement.

"I look what?" she choked.

"You know, Les, you really do." Apparently Terry must have noticed the outrage in Lesley's flashing blue eyes.

"That what Daniels said." She grew angry all over again.

"Is that what you're so hot about?" Terry quizzed her with open curiosity.

This was probably the first time in several years that Lesley was reluctant to share something with her sister. They'd always been close, but she felt a strange reluctance to tell Terry about Cole Daniels.

"That and more." She realized her attitude was absurd. Terry was her sister. So, as unemotionally as possible, Lesley related the events of the evening.

But to her dismay both Terry and Robert burst out laughing at Cole's comment that he would pray for her. Their amusement did little to ease her indignation. Lesley found nothing in her situation worthy of laughter. Pinching her mouth tightly shut, she moved into the crowd and joined the others in a song fest.

Later, the awards for the best costume were given, and Lesley won for the most original. Her smile was tremulous as she accepted the hand-crafted bow and submitted to a series of picture taking. But the pleasure of the award didn't show in her eyes, and she felt drained and tired by the time the party broke up shortly before ten.

Robert and Terry walked out to the parking lot with her. Robert ran a hand along her car bumper. "It hardly shows. Of course, it's hard to tell without daylight. But by the look of things, you got off lightly."

"I suppose." Lesley knew she didn't sound grateful, but Cole Daniels had ruined her evening.

Terry gave her a funny look that Lesley chose to ignore.

"It's been a long week." Robert exchanged glances with his wife, but not before Lesley caught a glimpse of censure in their eyes.

"Yes, it has," Lesley agreed. "Tomorrow I'm going to look through the want ads and see about finding someplace to move. I can't take much more of that ill-mannered creep from next door."

Lesley saw Terry open her mouth, then just as quickly close it.

"You might sleep on it," Robert advised.

"I might," she said more sharply then she intended. "I'll see you tomorrow." The comment was directed to Terry. The sisters did their errands and grocery shopping together on Saturdays.

"Night." Lesley scooted inside her car and started the engine.

"Night." Robert answered for them both.

Lesley noticed that her sister and brother-in-law were engaged in a lively conversation on the way back into the church. After a minute, Terry's head bobbed in agreement. Unconcerned, Lesley drove home. She would move. It was the perfect solution. There was no need to live this far out of town. But then she did enjoy the country life and having a large garden.

Lesley recalled how she and Terry had found

the duplex shortly after Terry was married. She remembered the pride they had in painting the house and tilling the backyard for the garden. The closeness they'd shared as sisters had been enhanced because they lived so near to each other.

Now everything was different, thanks to Cole Daniels.

His car was in the driveway when she pulled up. Although she felt like slamming the car door, she exercised rigid restraint and allowed it to shut normally. She was reaching across her seat for the empty cookie plate and her purse when he spoke.

"I see you made it home safely."

Cole was leaning indolently against his doorjamb, his arms and legs crossed as he regarded her with lazy indulgence.

Lesley stiffened and swallowed back an angry outburst. "Yes, I did," she said tautly, her voice tight, "no thanks to you."

"I sent the tow truck." His mouth deepened into grooves as he fought to suppress a smile.

"Am I supposed to thank you for that?"

"A little appreciation wouldn't be amiss."

Hands on hips, she glared at him across the short distance that separated them. "Well, thank you very much."

"You're welcome."

"You . . . you left me standing out there in the

dark and alone. I was worried sick. Because of you I missed half the party and the whole thing was your fault in the first place and—"

"My, my," he interrupted, the lazy smile evident in his voice. "You've worked yourself into a regular snit."

"Don't you dare say that word to me!" She pointed her index finger at him accusingly. "You left me there. Anything could have happened after you drove off." She could see that her anger was affecting him.

Cole straightened, dropping his hands to his side. "And just what was I supposed to do?" he challenged, an impatient edge to his voice.

"Help me!" she shouted.

"You needed a tow truck. I'm not Superman— I can't lift cars out of ditches."

"But . . . but you told the driver you thought I was a weirdo."

"From what I've witnessed this past week, who could argue?"

"You're the most despicable, selfish and hurtful man I've ever known. If I never saw you again I'd—"

"And you've got to be the most unreasonable, childish—"

"I don't have to stand here and listen to this garbage," Lesley shouted and whirled around. She stormed up the steps to her front door and turned the knob. Nothing. She tried again,

65

pushing it in with her shoulder, forgetting she had locked it.

"Don't tell me I have to come over and hold your hand while you open the door?"

Lesley tossed him a look that left little doubt of what she was thinking. Her hand shook as she inserted the key into the lock. Cole Daniels had to be the most irritating man she had ever encountered. This little incident was the crack that broke the dam. She'd move. Tomorrow first thing she'd start looking for another apartment.

Still keyed up, Lesley jerked the cone from the top of her head and paced the living room floor like a wild, caged animal. The impatient tap that sounded from his side of the wall only fueled her anger. With purpose-filled steps she strode over and pounded right back. Take that, she fumed.

She changed out of her costume and climbed into a full-length purple velvet robe. Never had she reacted like this to any man, any situation. Not only did her personality grate against Cole's, he had the ability to make her say and do things that were normally foreign to her gentle nature.

The muted tapping sounds of the typewriter came through the walls. Did Cole feel the same way about her?

Lesley brought her knees up, hugging them against her stomach as she rested her chin on top.

Did she resent him because he'd taken her

sister's place? The thought was too ridiculous to even consider.

The irritating blast of a car horn came from outside. Lesley stood and pulled back the center of the closed drapes to see what was happening.

A sinking sensation attacked the pit of her stomach and shut her eyes as frustration burned its way through her. This evening was going from bad to worse.

The car horn blared again impatiently as Dale and Frank drove onto the lawn, their tires digging deep into the damp grass.

Behind the small crack separating the drapes, Lesley watched as Dale climbed out of the passenger side of the car. He staggered a little, paused and took a long swig from the beer bottle he was carrying.

The doorbell buzzed and Lesley stared at the wooden door with terrified eyes. She wouldn't answer it.

"Come on, baby," Dale cooed. "I know you're inside. We've got a party to go to."

Frozen in a standing position by the window, Lesley could hear her heart pounding in a wild beat. Nothing had ever sounded so loud. Dale was sure to hear it. Should she phone the police? Would Frank and Dale hear her movements inside the apartment and break down the door if she did? What did she have handy that she could defend herself with?

"Don't let her get away with this," Lesley heard Frank shout out the car window. "Put your foot down, man," he added.

Dale jabbed the doorbell a second time, then started pounding furiously against the front door.

In desperation, Lesley hurried into the kitchen and phoned the police station. She couldn't deal with two drunks, and there was no telling what could happen.

The officer who answered kept Lesley on the line for several minutes, taking down the necessary information. He assured her a patrol car was on the way.

When Lesley returned to the living room, she could hear angry shouts. Another glance out the window confirmed her suspicions. Cole was on the front lawn demanding that Frank and Dale leave. Frank had climbed out of the car and appeared to be the more sober of the two as he approached Cole, his look dark and angry.

The argument was fast becoming heated, the language more abusive. When Dale took a wild swing at Cole, Lesley gave a small cry of alarm. Cole ducked but took a punch in the stomach from Frank. Dumbfounded, Lesley stared as Cole stumbled a few steps before recovering enough to fight off Dale, who was attempting to hold him down so Frank could punch him.

More outraged then she could remember

being in her life, Lesley grabbed the broom from the kitchen and stalked outside.

"Get out of here," she shouted at Dale and brushing him across the chest with the straw part of the broom. She repeated the action again and again, her revulsion fueling the attack.

Dale brought up his hands to defend himself, then tried to grab the broom out of her hand. He caught the bristly part and was pulling her to him when Cole laid him flat with one well-delivered blow. Frank was already on the grass, apparently knocked out.

"Are you all right?" Cole asked her breathlessly, his shoulders heaving. An ugly bruise was forming along the side of his face, and the knuckles on one hand were beginning to swell.

"I'm fine. What about you?"

He nodded and wiped the side of his mouth with the back of his hand.

A silence settled between them as they regarded each other.

Unsure, she lifted her hand, her fingertips lightly brushing the hair from his temple, and explored the darkening bruise.

Cole's smoldering gaze ran over her face, and their eyes locked. His look was gentle yet intense, and Lesley felt weak, as if her knees were about to give out on her.

A gentle smile touched his mouth. "Four karate lessons and you come at him with a broom?"

"I took the first thing that came to mind." There was a breathlessness to her response. "I didn't want you hurt because of Dale."

"Your friends?" His eyes narrowed slightly.

"Not likely." She shook her head self-consciously and looked away. "I went out with Dale a couple of times, but that was it."

Another car could be heard approaching, and simultaneously they turned to see who was coming. The police patrol car could be seen coming up the hill toward them.

"I called," Lesley supplied. "I didn't know what else to do." Was she imagining things, or did Cole tense and take a step in retreat?

"I don't want to become involved." His eyes seemed to bore into hers. "Agreed?"

Numbly Lesley nodded. Not become involved. But he already was. What he wanted was to avoid any contact with the police. But why?

By the time the two uniformed officers had parked their vehicle and approached her, Cole was inside the duplex, door closed and lights off. She cast one fleeting glance toward him, then turned her attention to the policemen.

The first one tipped his hat back with the end of his pencil. "Seems like you carry a mean broom, lady."

"Yes." Lesley swallowed tightly. "These two are drunk and disorderly."

The second officer picked up an empty beer can

beside the car. "I think we get the picture. Looks like their car may have ruined a portion of your yard."

"Are you going to arrest them?"

"Looks that way. Any qualms?"

"None." Lesley's hand clenched the broom handle. "Throw the book at them."

"You'll need to answer a few questions."

The first officer returned to the police car and picked up the microphone to his radio.

"Would you mind coming down to the station and answering a few questions?" he asked, surveying the two men, who were sitting up. Dale was rubbing the side of his jaw and looked around confused. Frank was out cold.

"No," she agreed meekly, "I don't mind at all. Let me change and I'll be there in a few minutes."

"This one says a man slugged him." The officer glanced at Lesley.

"Ask him about ghosts and goblins—he probably saw those too," Lesley supplied. She wouldn't lie outright, but she owed Cole a debt of appreciation. "I'll be right back, Officer."

After an hour and a half at the police station, Lesley parked her car in the driveway to her apartment. Halloween wasn't a holiday she'd soon forget if as much happened to her every year. She felt bone-weary. It seemed that in the space of a few hours more had happened in her life than the past twenty years.

When her car door slammed, Cole came out of his duplex. His tall figure filled the open doorway, silhouetted by the light. "Everything go okay?"

"Fine." She wiped a hand across her face and sighed. "Frank and Dale are sleeping it off in the drunk tank." At his concerned look she added, "Neither one of them even showed signs of a struggle. I think you got the worse end of that deal." The bruise on his face looked angry and she squelched feelings of guilt. "Would . . . would you like a cup of cocoa?" She wasn't sure why she issued the invitation. Tonight he had made her angrier than anyone or anything and only a short time later had rescued her from what could have been a nasty scene. The invitation was a way of extending her hand in friendship, her way of saying "Let bygones be bygones."

Cole hesitated, and Lesley tensed. He knew what she was saying. Now she almost regretted having asked. "Look, I didn't ask for your hand in marriage. A decision shouldn't be that difficult."

"You must be exhausted." He was offering her an excuse.

She refused it. "No, I'm too keyed up to sleep."

With a dignified jut of her chin, she stood back and waited. She became fascinated with his strong profile as he stood in the open door. The contrast between Dale and Cole was all the more striking. There wasn't anything artificial about

Cole. He was all male . . . and distant. Did he want to keep it that way?

His expression changed, softening somewhat. "Another time, perhaps."

Lesley sucked in a hurt breath. He was refusing her? She had extended an appreciative hand of friendship and he rejected it. It hurt. That was what surprised her. He turned her down and she felt like an insecure teen who hadn't been asked to the prom.

"Good night, Lesley." He turned back into his apartment and closed the door.

Was that regret she heard in his voice? Nibbling on the corner of her bottom lip, Lesley walked into her half of the duplex. Although dark and filled with shadows from a three-quarter moon, her home offered comfort and security.

Slipping off her shoes, Lesley flexed her toes in the carpet before moving into the kitchen and flipping on a light switch. Immediately the area was bathed in a soft glow.

She opened the refrigerator, took out a carton of milk and poured herself a glass. The package of hamburger caught her attention as she returned the milk carton.

Not giving herself the opportunity to change her mind, she slipped back into her shoes and marched over to Cole's front door.

He answered after the first knock, his expression thoughtful as his eyes fell on the meat.

"Here." She gave him the hamburger.

"Thanks, but I've already had dinner."

"It's not to eat," she announced primly. "Put it over your bruise."

A smile quivered at the corners of his sensuous mouth. "I thought you were supposed to use steak for that?"

"I didn't have steak, only hamburger," Lesley reasoned.

"I'm afraid I could only accept Choice, Grade A tenderloin beef. Corn-fed preferred." A teasing quality crept into his voice.

"Honestly," she admonished, quickly losing the fragile grip on her temper, "just take the hamburger. It'll make me feel better so I can get some sleep."

"And if you're asleep, you can't bother me," he added as if that was enough of an inducement for him to take the meat.

"Exactly," she said a trifle flippantly.

" 'Tis done. Good night, Lesley, for the third time."

"Good riddance, you mean," she muttered with a brash air of unconcern.

His chuckle followed her as she turned and began to walk away.

"Lesley."

Expectantly she turned around.

His gaze flickered over her and she watched as a muscle in his jaw tensed. "Nothing. Good night."

Chapter Four

Lesley lay on her back, her hands supporting her head as she stared at the dark ceiling. Sleep was impossible.

The sounds of the typewriter had stopped, but Cole wasn't asleep either. She could hear his movements on the other side of the wall. It sounded as if he was pacing: walking to one side of the small living room, pivoting and strolling back . . . again and again and again.

Lesley closed her eyes, and the mental image of Cole formed in her mind. He looked troubled and weary; at least, that was how she'd seen him last. She wondered what he'd done with the hamburger. The thought was silly.

The pacing stopped and the night grew silent. But Lesley couldn't sleep. About three, she tossed back the covers and climbed out of bed. She never did have that glass of milk. Maybe it would help now.

The small lamp on the end table in the living room was all the light she needed. Holding the milk glass, she sat on the sofa and brought her knees up so she could slip the warm gown over her feet. The Bible she used for devotions sat beside the lamp. Idly Lesley flipped through the pages. Her parents had given her this purse-size edition when she turned sixteen. The pages were dog-eared, the edges worn from years of use. Important pieces of her life were tucked away in its flap: the newspaper notice of her grand-mother's death, a small card from Terry and Robert's wedding and Lisa's birth announcement.

Long ago Lesley had learned that if she couldn't sleep, reading God's Word had a sooth-ing effect on her. Opening the book at random, she was surprised to see that it opened at Matthew, Chapter 22. Usually her Bible opened to Psalms, since that book was directly in the middle.

The bold-phrased lettering seemed to jump off the page at her. A soft smile touched her face. You shall love the Lord your God with all your heart, and with all your soul, and with all your mind. The greatest commandment. Lesley had read these words a hundred times, but the second part of the commandment caused a tightening sensation in her throat. You shall love your neighbor as yourself.

Lesley closed the book and laid her head against the back of the couch. Love thy neighbor. Was this coincidence, or was God giving her a special message? But if He was sending her something with a profound meaning, it would be preceded by a blare from trumpets, or at least an angel's announcement. Not His word in the still of a sleepless night. Love thy neighbor, her thoughts reiterated. Cole Daniels had not been an error. God had sent him to her. Lesley didn't know why, nor did she question. For now she would trust. But sometimes that was the hardest thing to do.

"I just can't believe it." Terry looped a strand of hair around her ear and pushed the grocery cart ahead so another shopper could get by.

"I find Dale's behavior just as unbelievable," Lesley returned, placing several red Delicious apples in a cellophane bag.

"I didn't think he'd do anything like that. You're not still thinking about moving, are you?"

"No." Lesley looked up, startled for a moment. She'd forgotten she'd even threatened as much yesterday. "Not anymore." Although she hadn't told her sister about Cole's intervention with Dale and Frank, after last night she felt assured God had her exactly where she was supposed to be.

"Didn't your neighbor hear any of the commotion?" Terry feigned engrossment in the Delicious apples.

Amused at her sister's interest, Lesley successfully stifled a smile. Terry had an apple tree in her backyard, and the two had spent one whole

77

weekend picking fruit and canning applesauce.

"I'm sure he did."

"And?" Terry prompted.

"And the police arrived." Her fingers gripping the handle of the cart, Lesley pushed it farther down the crowded aisle.

"But you don't think you'll move?" Terry sounded relieved.

"I did a lot of thinking about it last night and decided that maybe God hadn't made such a horrendous mistake after all."

"I'm sure He didn't."

"I'm even beginning to believe there's a reason God moved Cole Daniels beside me."

"I think there is."

Lesley paused long enough to turn around, her laughing eyes studying her sister. "Has anyone ever told you that on rare occasions you sound like a parrot?"

Terry batted her eyelashes wickedly. "Polly want a cracker."

They both giggled like carefree friends and continued with their shopping.

After Halloween night, Cole avoided Lesley. She didn't see him for days, and once when she made up an excuse to knock at his door, he didn't answer. It was almost as if the duplex hadn't been rented. However, she knew he was there. And even though they didn't communicate, her awareness of him grew. She discovered that her early morning prayers often included Cole, and later recognized that he was dominating her thoughts more and more.

The first snowfall of the year came the second week in November. Lesley woke early and responded with delight to the fluffy white flakes that drifted to the earth like goose down descending from some glorious heaven. Her excitement dissipated with the knowledge that she had to dress and get into town. Although only a few inches covered the ground, the white powder was falling thick and heavy. She could have trouble getting out of the driveway.

After a hurried shower, Lesley dressed in dark wool pants and a thick pink ski sweater. The snow shovel was in the storage shed in the back of the apartment with the garden equipment. Tying a scarf around her neck, she next slipped on her knee-high boots and opened the sliding glass door to retrieve the shovel.

Halfway across the backyard, she noticed another pair of fresh footprints in the snow: a larger foot that made deep impressions in the fallen crystalline purity. Cole's, Lesley mused.

The shovel was missing. Blowing on her bare hands with her warm breath and rubbing them together, Lesley came around the side of the house to find Cole busy shoveling the snow from the driveway.

"Morning," she called, more than a little pleased to see him again. He looked well. His hair needed cutting, and the bronze tan that had caused her to wonder at his penchant for the indoors had faded. But he looked vibrant, fit and all male.

Cole stopped shoveling and straightened. "I didn't think I'd catch you up this early."

In other words, he'd been hoping to get away without seeing her at all.

A smile broke out across her face as she ignored his lack of welcome. "You don't need to do that." He was clearing the area behind her car so that she could back out safely.

He scraped the shovel against the cement and threw the snow aside. "I know that."

"Were you afraid that if I got snowed in, I'd be around to pester you all day?"

He paused momentarily. "You could say that."

That was a rotten thing to say. For days she'd taken pains to stay out of his way. If he didn't want to see her, that was fine. At least, that was what she'd been telling herself.

"Cole?" With an innocent lilt to her voice she called his name, mischief glittering from her eyes.

He glanced up expectantly just as Lesley threw the snowball and hit him squarely in the chest.

"How could I possibly bother you?" she challenged. "I haven't seen you in weeks." Her hands rested defiantly on slim hips; her eyes sparkled brightly.

For an instant Cole looked stunned. "So much for Christian charity," he murmured and tossed the shovel aside.

Lesley couldn't keep from laughing. Stooping over, she packed a second snowball. "You seem to think I'll let you get away with insulting me. Ha!"

Cole leaned over and formed his own snowball as a smile slowly made its way across his face. "How did I insult you?" he asked in a danger-ously calm voice.

Her bare hands were freezing and she tossed her threat to the ground and rubbed the warmth back into her frozen fingers. "Peace?" she asked hopefully.

"Oh no, you started this."

"But . . . I don't have any gloves on."

"You knew that when you threw the first snowball."

"But . . ." For every step he took toward her, Lesley took one in retreat. "Would it help if I apologized?"

"It might," he said and advanced another threatening step. "And then again, it might not."

"You wouldn't."

"Don't challenge me, Lesley." His mirthful eyes pinned her.

"But you shouldn't have said that."

"Said what?"

"That I pester you."

"You haven't stopped since the day I first saw you."

"That's not true," she cried indignantly.

"You have no way of knowing, my blue-eyed temptress."

With bubbling laughter, she reached down, grabbed her snowball and threw it at him with remarkable accuracy. Intense satisfaction raced through her when she saw she'd caught him completely off guard. Pivoting sharply, she ran toward the house. Ten steps from her front door, Cole caught her.

Lesley let out a squeal as his hands gripped her upper arms and flung her around. Somehow she managed to elude him, but Cole made a diving catch for her that sent them both crashing to the snow.

Laughing and breathless, she tossed her head to and fro as Cole attempted to hold her face. "I'm sorry," she cried with bubbling exhilaration.

"I just bet you are."

"I'll never do it again, I promise."

Cole was lying halfway on top of her, his hands pinning hers above her head. Her deep smiling eyes met his as she heaved a giant breath from her lungs.

The warm, smoldering light clashed with hers, and they both went still. Slowly the laughter faded from him. Lesley noted that his gaze slid to her mouth, and it was all she could do not to moisten her lips in eager anticipation. He was so close that all she had to do was lift her head. His mouth hovered above hers for a timeless moment.

Lesley lowered her lashes, hungry for the taste of this man who had haunted her for weeks.

The hold on her hands relaxed and Lesley's gaze shot to Cole as he stood and brushed the snow from his pant legs. Resting her weight on her elbows, Lesley sat up and stared at him dumbfoundedly. When he extended a hand to her, she placed her bare one in his and was lifted from the wet snow.

Her eyes were filled with questions, but he ignored them. Cool and aloof, he pushed her toward the stairs into the apartment. "Get dressed or you'll be late for work."

"Yes sir," she tossed back saucily.

A hint of a grin sprang into his eyes and just as quickly disappeared. "I'll finish digging you out."

She stood, one foot resting on the porch, the other on the top step. "Cole."

He turned.

"Thanks."

"Why thank me?" he said in a husky voice. "I'm doing this for completely selfish reasons."

The words were meant to disarm her, and they did. With a sad smile, Lesley retreated into the warmth of her home.

Snow was a part of life in northern Idaho, but the first snowfall of the year created the usual rush on the service stations for snow tires and chains. Lesley bypassed the station where she normally did business and instead stopped in at Paul Walker's on her way home. After filling her gas tank, she stepped into the resort grocery.

"Howdy, Paul," she called out cheerfully. It was just after four-thirty, and already the sun was beginning to set. Heavy clouds darkened the sky. "Looks like we're due for more snow."

"Seems that way." Paul was stacking jars of peanut butter on the shelf. "Anything I can get you?"

"How about a snowplow?"

He chuckled good-naturedly. "Haven't seen your neighbor in quite a while. Must be a week or so since the last time he was in. Buys most of his things here. Even had me special-order a few things I didn't have handy."

"Cole Daniels?"

"Only close neighbor you got up your way, I'd say."

Cole had continued to do his main shopping in this resort store? Groceries were 20 percent cheaper in town.

"In fact, if it isn't too much trouble, would you mind taking him a couple of things? He paid for them. No need to let them sit around here with you being so close and all."

"No," Lesley answered thoughtfully, "I don't mind."

"Good." Paul returned his attention to the peanut butter, and Lesley strolled down the narrow aisles picking up coarse salt and the latest issue of *TV Guide.*

Paul handed her a small sack marked "Daniels" after she paid for the gas and the couple of things she'd gotten.

Her thoughts were as heavy as the gray clouds that obliterated the sky when Lesley drove home. The hill had been sanded, which made the access up the hill to her place easier.

What did Cole do for a living? He was always there—at least, his car was. He seldom came out of doors. Sometimes she had the feeling he was hiding. But why, and from whom? She'd tried to tell Terry her suspicions on several occasions, but Terry had laughed them off, attributing such ideas to Lesley's overactive imagination. Rather than argue, Lesley said nothing.

Cole's lights were on when she pulled into her driveway. After dropping off her sack in the kitchen, she walked over to his front door. He didn't respond to her first rap.

"Come on, Cole," she cried, half-angry. What did he think she was going to do? "I promise I don't have any snowballs."

The sound of his chuckle could be heard before he unlatched the lock and pulled open his door.

"Paul Walker sent this along." She gave him the small sack. The temptation to take a look had been almost overwhelming, but she'd resisted. Lesley hated to think of herself as the nosy type.

Frowning, Cole took the sack, looked inside, then glanced up at her. "Was there something else you wanted?" he asked dryly.

Why was it Cole had the ability to make her feel like a repentant child? "No, there's nothing else," she shot back hotly. She pivoted and marched down the steps.

"Lesley," he called out, stopping her.

She turned back, her eyes flashing angry signals at him.

"Thanks."

"You're welcome." She didn't feel the least bit gracious. She'd done him a favor, and Cole acted as if she'd purposely intruded on his privacy. "Next time I won't bother," she mumbled under her breath as she righteously marched back to her half of the duplex.

"Maybe you shouldn't," Cole called after her.

Lesley closed the door, the light and warmth of her home welcoming her. She wasn't angry with Cole, but more puzzled than anything. She didn't understand him, and the more she tried, the more confused she became.

Lesley opened a can of stew and let it warm on

the stove while she changed into her wool pants and sweater. The phone rang as she reappeared in the kitchen.

"Hello," she answered and stirred the bubbling meat and vegetables.

"Hi, how's it going?"

It was her sister. "Fine."

"Have any trouble getting to work this morning?"

"No. Cole helped dig me out."

"That was nice."

"Neighborly, but I think he had his own interests at heart. If I was home, I might find out what he does with his time all day."

"Honestly, Les, are you still on that kick?" Terry asked and heaved a sigh. "I sometimes think you missed your calling in life. You should be working for the FBI."

"Maybe," Lesley decided not to argue.

"I got a letter from Mom and Dad today." Their parents wintered in Arizona every year.

"Oh, what did Mom have to say?"

"The usual. They're having a good time, Dad's golfing every day and enjoying himself. They wanted to know if all of us would come down for Christmas. Robert's going to see if he can get off an extra day, but you know what the post office is like this time of year. It looks doubtful for us. What about you?"

"I . . . I don't know yet, I'll have to check the schedule at the bank." The lights flickered, then dimmed. "It looks like I may be losing my electricity. What's happening your way?"

"Nothing yet, but you can bet if you go, we will."

"I'd better get off the phone and look for a candle. I'll talk to you tomorrow."

"Okay."

The soft buzz of the receiver told Lesley her sister had hung up.

Lesley was opening a kitchen drawer when the lights flickered a second time just before everything went completely dark. "Rats," she blurted out impatiently, fumbling to locate the flashlight in the kitchen junk drawer. Her fingers encountered something sharp, and she inhaled a pain-filled breath and jerked out her hand. The abrupt action pulled the drawer out of its socket and dumped the contents on the floor in a tremendous crash.

Something crashed on the toe of her slipper and Lesley cried out more from shock than pain.

Within seconds Cole was pounding on her sliding glass door. When she didn't immediately respond, he pushed it aside and flashed a light across the floor.

"Lesley," he asked anxiously, "are you all right?"

"I . . . I think so."

"What happened?"

"I was trying to find a flashlight and the drawer fell."

"Why are you sucking your finger?"

"Because it's bleeding."

"Let me see." He maneuvered his way through the mess on the floor and took her hand.

"It's fine. I think I caught it on the end of an open pocketknife."

"Serves you right," he admonished gently.

A tingling warmth was spreading up to her elbow from his gentle but firm touch. He set the flashlight on the counter and turned the palm of her hand over to better examine the small cut. "It doesn't look too bad. Have any bandages handy?"

"The bathroom," she supplied.

The flashlight on the counter dimmed and within seconds had faded completely.

"Oh, great."

"No need to panic," Cole muttered with an edge of impatience.

"I'm not panicking," she denied. "I'll get mine. It should be down here somewhere." She took a tentative step and her foot encountered a spool of thread. "Oh," she gasped and flung her hands out to catch herself.

Cole wrapped his arms around her waist and caught her just as she started to fall. "It's dangerous just being around you."

Lesley's senses were clamoring at his nearness, and she required a couple of seconds to recover from the impact of being held by Cole.

Cole was just as affected. Lesley could feel

the battle that seemed to be going on inside him. He tensed and inhaled deeply; his warm breath fanned the side of her face near her temple.

Lesley didn't swallow, didn't move. Instinct demanded that she turn into his arms, but she resisted. Her throat felt dry and scratchy.

"Lesley." He murmured her name softly. His arms turned so that only a few scant inches separated them. Gently a finger caressed her cheek and wandered to her lips in sweet, burning exploration.

Softly she moaned at the pure pleasure of his touch. "Cole." His name came in the form of a husky whisper.

His hand curved around the back of her neck, tilting her head up to meet his descending mouth.

Lesley released a slow sigh as she slipped her hands up to rest on the muscular curve of his shoulders. Her lips parted in response as he kissed her. Joyfully her heart burst into a wild, welcoming song.

The contact deepened as Cole pulled her tighter against him. The melody continued as he kissed her again and again in jubilant reprise. Lesley locked her arms around his neck. It felt so right, so good. She'd been kissed before, but not like this. Never had she wanted anything more than to be held by Cole.

Abruptly his hands closed over her wrists and

firmly pulled her free. His fingers continued to grip hers.

Lesley's eyes had adjusted to the darkness, and she noted the harsh twist of Cole's mouth.

"That shouldn't have happened."

Was that regret she heard? "You kissed me," she whispered, her voice low and slightly shaky. "It's not that big a deal." She strove to sound flippant and unaffected.

"You don't understand." He raked his fingers through the tousled dark hair.

"No, I don't."

He lifted a dark strand from her face and kissed her again, lightly, brushing her lips with a sweet intensity that made her yearn for more.

"See?"

"See what?" she mumbled, still trapped in the rapture of his kiss.

"Once will never do. Kissing you, holding you will only make me yearn for more. I can't get involved with a woman. Not now. You couldn't possibly understand." His hands roamed up and down her back as if he couldn't bring himself to break away.

"No, I don't," Lesley admitted. "But I know that I like the feel of this." Standing on the tips of her toes, her hands on his shoulders, she pressed her mouth ardently over his.

Cole groaned and pulled her closer, kissing her long and hard.

Lesley broke the pressure and nestled her head

to his chest, a gentle smile curving the corners of her mouth. She didn't know what was troubling Cole, but for now he cared more about holding her. A feeling of triumph filled her. Her mouth throbbed from his kisses, and his ragged breath stirred the short tendrils at the side of her face.

"Lesley, we've got to talk."

"No." She kissed his strong neck. "If we talk, you'll push me away. And you've pushed me away for a long time, Cole Daniels."

"Be reasonable."

"How can I?"

His foot swung out and cleared a path so that they could move into the living room. The only light in the room came from the moon, and it was nearly impossible to maneuver in the darkness.

"Here," Lesley said, a smile evident in her voice. "Let me lead. At least I know where the couch is."

"I know where everything is in this apartment," he muttered in a husky tone.

"How?"

"Don't you realize I can hear you? Some nights you drove me crazy. I'd picture you . . ." He paused and expelled his breath. "Never mind."

They sat, and immediately Cole looped his arm around her shoulder, bringing her close to his side. One hand slid around his ribs and she pressed her face to his solid chest.

"Cole," she said, not knowing where to begin, "tell me what you're doing here."

She felt him stiffen.

"What do you mean . . . doing here?"

"You don't have a job. How do you support yourself?"

"Because you allow a man to kiss you, does that give you the right to interrogate him?"

"No. Forget I asked, I don't care."

"Right now, with you in my arms, I don't either." The words were spoken so low that Lesley had to strain to hear him.

Afraid to ask anything more, Lesley didn't speak, content to be in his arms. After a while she realized by the even fall and rise of his chest that Cole had fallen asleep. Sometimes she wondered when he slept. No matter when she was up, early morning or late at night, so was Cole. Several times when she'd happened to catch a glimpse of him, she thought he was a man who had driven himself to the limits of his endurance. Now, in her arms, he slept peacefully.

Even when the lights came back on, Cole didn't stir. Lesley disentangled herself from his embrace, gently placed his head on a decorator pillow from the end of the sofa and covered him with a blanket.

She picked up the contents of the drawer and replaced it in the slot. Another hour passed before she ate the beef stew that had been simmering on the stove. Still Cole didn't stir.

In repose he looked like a lost and troubled

youth. His forehead was creased in deep-grooved lines, his mouth tight, his body tense even in sleep.

Carrying her dish to the sink, Lesley turned, her hands gripping the edge of the counter behind her. As her gaze rested on Cole, a prayer came to her. Maybe someday he'd feel confident enough to share what was troubling him with her, but for now she must be content with the progress she had made. The thick wall of anger and bitterness he had erected against her and the world was gradually being lowered. Tonight was the beginning, just the beginning.

Lesley was running the water into the sink to do the dinner dishes when Cole stirred. He jerked himself upright and looked around.

Drying her hands on a terry-cloth towel, Lesley walked into the living room. "I must say this is the first time I've had that effect on a man."

He looked at her blankly, then bounded to his feet and ran his hand along the side of his head. "I should never have come here."

"But you did and I'm glad."

His eyes narrowed menacingly. "Just because I kissed you, it doesn't give you the right to—"

"I don't expect a thing," she assured him softly. "Are you hungry?"

"No." He sounded disconcerted, angry.

"Cole, what's wrong?" she probed gently.

"Wrong?" he snapped. "Everything's wrong. I was a fool to come here."

"But, Cole—"

"Listen, Miss Do Right," he said, pointing an accusing finger in her direction, "I knew you were trouble the minute I laid eyes on you."

"That's interesting," she countered evenly. "I felt the same thing about you." Not until tonight did she acknowledge that what they'd experienced was attraction, one so powerful and explosive it could disrupt their entire lives.

"I don't want you in my life. Can I be more blunt than that?" He stalked to the far side of the room, his back to her.

A lump was growing in her throat, making it difficult to swallow. "No, I don't think you can."

"Is it possible for us to live side by side and stay out of each other's way?" Still he kept his back to her.

"Yes," she mumbled. "Go on and go. I don't know why you're running, and I don't care. But I'll be here waiting when you're through."

He turned to her then, his eyes dark and tormented. She yearned to go to him and erase the lines of indecision and anguish, but she stood still and silent.

His hand gripped the doorknob, and she watched as his knuckles turned white. He didn't want to leave, but some force stronger than anything she could inspire in him drove him away and into the silent night.

Chapter Five

Lesley didn't see Cole for another week. Their meeting then was by chance. She'd gone down to the mailbox to collect her mail and saw a deer in the distance. It was unusual for the animals to come down this far, but already winter had been harsh and undoubtedly the small deer had been searching for food. Not wanting to frighten the lovely tan-skinned creature, she moved cautiously, following it into the wooded area behind the duplex. To her surprise, she found that a bale of hay had been spread out and two other deer were eating from it.

Out of the corner of her eye, Lesley happened to catch a movement. She turned and saw Cole breaking apart another bale farther up the incline in the back of the property. Apparently he felt her presence and turned. Only a few yards separated them. Cole stopped and buried the pitchfork into the snow, his gaze never leaving hers.

"Hello, Lesley."

"Cole." She felt mesmerized by his gaze. He

looked tired, and she yearned to go to him. But she stood as she was, waiting, for what she didn't know.

"How have you been?"

She wanted to scream at him that she was miserable and that having him so close and yet so far away was hurting her unbearably. She longed to tell him that she knew he wasn't sleeping, because she wasn't sleeping either and could hear his movements. Some nights she pressed her fingertips to the wall because it was the only way she knew to communicate with him.

Lesley lowered her gaze. "I'm fine. And you?"

"Fine."

How could they lie to each other like this? She snapped her head up, suddenly angry. "If you won't be honest, then I will be. I'm miserable. I'd give anything to have the electricity go out again just so I could find that warm, vibrant man I was beginning to know." And love, her thoughts concluded.

A muscle twitched in Cole's jaw. "He doesn't exist."

"Don't tell me that," she cried. "I felt his arms around me, I know his touch and I. . . I gave him comfort. But when the lights came back—"

"When the lights returned," Cole interrupted angrily, "there was only me. I told you that night I should never have kissed you."

"But you did, and things have changed."

"They haven't," Cole argued. "They can't, I won't let them."

"You go ahead and try to deny it, then." The words trembled from her as she knotted her hands into tight fists. "Because I can't, and I've tried as hard as I can."

She turned and ran back to the apartment, her lower lip quivering as she slid the back door closed. Her whole body was shaking when she tossed the few pieces of mail on the table, her fingers biting into the back of the old kitchen chair.

Taking in several deep, calming breaths, Lesley put the teakettle on to boil. Would this be her fate, loving Cole? There hadn't been a time in her life that she felt more frustrated with anyone. And yet there was no reason she should love Cole: he was arrogant, stubborn, angry and hurtful. But the sensations he aroused in her were almost overpowering. There was something profound and intense about him. He was hiding from her and from the world. She might never know or understand him, but that didn't seem to matter to her heart.

When Lesley met her sister an hour later to do their weekly shopping, it was Terry who brought up the subject of Cole. They'd stopped in a local café for a quick lunch.

"Seen much of your neighbor lately?"

"Can't say that I have." Lesley attempted to brush aside her sister's interest.

"You know, for all the times you've talked about him, I've never seen him."

"I don't imagine you will. He's . . . private." She didn't know how else to explain it.

"Other than the first days he was in town, no one else has seen him except Paul Walker and you."

Lesley had mentioned the same thing only last week.

"I was wondering if you were safe up there with him."

"Very safe."

"But he could be an escaped convict."

Lesley didn't slough off Terry's sudden interest. "What makes you say something like that?"

Terry shrugged. "I don't know, but I started thinking about what you've been saying all these weeks and it doesn't add up, none of it."

"I'm not going to concern myself with it now."

"But he could be dangerous."

Now it was Lesley's turn to laugh. "Something isn't right with Cole Daniels, but I trust him implicitly. He'd never hurt me."

Terry set the fork she'd been fingering beside her untouched plate. "You're falling for this guy, aren't you?"

An immediate denial rose to Lesley's lips, but didn't make it past her nod of acknowledgment.

"Oh, Les," Terry groaned. "I was afraid of that."

"I'm a big girl now."

"Yes, I know, but I'd hate to see you get hurt."

"O, ye of little faith," Lesley said with a teasing smile. "Weren't you the one who was constantly telling me that we prayed about my new neighbor and that whoever God sent was—"

"Don't remind me," Terry interrupted, her voice filled with self-reproach. "But, Les, honestly, I'm worried about you."

"I don't know why you should be. If God sent Cole Daniels, then there's a reason. I don't know what it is yet, but I'm sure I will shortly."

"How can you sound so confident?"

Lesley fluttered her long lashes closed. "I'm not sure what Cole's running from, or if he's hiding at all. But I believe that he feels just as strongly about me."

Terry's round eyes brightened to a deeper shade of blue. "But I thought you hardly ever saw him and—"

"But I see the way he looks at me." Lesley glanced down at her chef's salad, idly fingering her napkin in her lap. "We've both been infected with the same virus."

"Love?" Terry made the word a haunting question. "But the kind meant to last a lifetime?"

"I don't know," Lesley returned sadly, "I simply don't know."

The conversation with her sister played back in Lesley's mind as she drove home. When she pulled into the driveway, she noted that something was different but couldn't put her finger on it until she'd taken the last bag of groceries into the apartment. Standing on the top step, she surveyed the area. Cole's car was missing. That was what was wrong.

Without meaning to, Lesley listened for his return the rest of the afternoon. Snow began falling again in soft feathery flakes that covered the ground. Several times Lesley found herself looking out the window. Not that she'd admit openly that she was watching for Cole . . . or anxious for him. Did he have car problems? Maybe he needed help.

Stop it, her mind shouted as she ran her fingers through the silky length of her hair. She was behaving like a worrisome mother. Cole could take care of himself.

About three, Lesley decided to bake cookies. She was ready to do anything to keep her mind off Cole. When she heard him enter the second half of the duplex, she released an unconscious sigh of relief.

Standing motionless in the kitchen, she heard him walk across the floor. Another pair of footsteps echoed and Lesley straightened. Someone was with him.

As quietly as possible, Lesley tiptoed into the living room and peeked out the window. Another car was parked in the driveway next to Cole's.

Her eyes narrowed in concentration. She'd seen that car before, but where? She bit into the corner of her mouth. Red and flashy, it . . . She stopped, her mind spinning in deep-grooved channels. That was the car Cole had driven the first day she'd met him—the one parked in the driveway the day he moved into the duplex. Where had it been all this time? What had he done with it?

While she was still musing over these thoughts, the sound of raised voices filtered through the wall opposite Lesley's living room.

"Engstrom, be reasonable. The one who's going to end up getting hurt in this is you. Do you have any idea how hard Jennings is looking for you?"

The man had called Cole "Engstrom." Had he been using a false name all these months?

"He'd never find me here. Coeur d'Alene, Idaho?"

Cole made it sound like the end of the earth.

"Maybe."

The mystery man didn't seem to echo Cole's confidence.

"How's the report coming?"

"I'm finished."

"Good grief, you must have half killed yourself to do it in this time."

A short silence followed.

"Take it with you. See to it that . . ."

The timer on the stove dinged and Lesley

yanked her attention to the kitchen. As quickly as possible she turned it off and took the cookie sheet out of the oven. The aroma of melting chocolate chips filled the small apartment.

Like a thief in the night, Lesley returned to the living room.

". . . low profile?"

"As much as possible," Cole said, "but the girl next door has guessed something isn't right."

The other man laughed. "But you've always had a way with women. I wouldn't worry about her."

"I'm not."

Was that displeasure Lesley heard in Cole's cool tones?

"Do you want me to get back to you?"

"When you can."

"Listen, Engstrom. Don't take any chances. Your life won't be worth a plug nickel if Jennings gets wind of your whereabouts."

"I won't."

Lesley's knees felt wobbly and weak. She lowered herself onto the couch and covered her mouth with one hand. Cole didn't need to worry about her suspicions. He could handle her. After all, he had a way with women.

More than that, he was in danger, terrible danger. Tears filled her eyes, blurring her vision. The two men continued talking, but Lesley couldn't make out what they were saying. A few minutes later she heard the front door open, then close. When she'd gathered the resolve to stand up and look out the window, the sporty red car was gone.

Lesley didn't eat dinner that night, and breakfast held no appeal the next morning as she dressed for church. She sat through the Sunday school and the morning worship service, but if anyone had asked her what had been discussed, Lesley couldn't have told them.

She talked and chatted with friends and promised to come to a baby shower the women's group was giving Jenny Perkins the following Tuesday. She smiled at the appropriate times, spoke when necessary, but her mind was buzzing and the sick feeling that had attacked the pit of her stomach yesterday afternoon persisted the rest of the day.

On her lunch break Monday afternoon, Lesley stopped in the library. She wasn't exactly sure what she was looking for, but she had a name and would go from there. Without arousing the librarian's curiosity, Lesley took down from the shelves several volumes relating to the auto industry. Twice she'd heard people say Cole seemed to know a lot about cars. The one remark that struck a chord of response in her had been that of the tow truck operator, who'd said Cole had fixed the foreign car after just listening to the engine.

Flipping through the indexes of several books, Lesley drew a blank.

"Can I help you?" The gray-haired librarian asked her when she returned an armload of books to the counter.

"Not today. Thanks."

Lesley returned at five after the bank had closed, took down several more volumes and sat at a table, leafing through the back pages.

"If you'd let me know what you're looking for I might be able to help." The librarian tried a second time.

"I have a name of someone and I wanted to see if I could find it. Someone who may have been in the news recently." It was a stab in the dark, but she didn't know where else to look. If Cole was running from the authorities, his name would have been in the newspapers.

The woman's brow was wrinkled in a deep frown. "Locally?"

"No, I was thinking more on a national level. Possibly from Indiana." That was where Cole's out-of-state check had been issued.

"Possibly the personal names in the New York Times Index would be of help, but we don't have that reference book here."

"Could you find out for me?"

The woman looked unsure. "I can check, but it may take a few days. What's the name?"

"Engstrom."

"First name?"

"I'm . . . not sure." If Daniels wasn't his last name, who was to know what he'd used for his first name?

"I probably won't have the information until the end of the week."

"That's fine. Thank you."

November and December were heavy snow months in northern Idaho. Normally Lesley didn't mind. Idaho was sometimes called America's Switzerland, and the skiing was fantastic—some of the world's best. But Lesley's thoughts weren't on the glacial valleys or the pristine forests as she pulled into her driveway.

Everything was still and beautiful. The town below looked like something out of a fairy tale. The sky was already dark, and Lesley's nerves were raw. She couldn't stay in the apartment without pacing, or having her stomach churn with nervous anxiety. What would she learn about Cole? What shocking thing was she about to uncover about the man she was coming to love so intensely, the stranger who lived next door?

With so much nervous energy pent up, Lesley charged out back and grabbed the snow shovel. Several inches more were forecast for the night. If she cleared the space behind her car now, it meant less work in the morning.

She had managed to shovel only a small portion of the area when Cole's front door slammed.

"Just what are you doing?" he demanded. His mood didn't appear to have improved.

Lesley straightened, one hand holding the shovel as she glared at Cole. She half expected him to look different, to have changed since their last meeting. He hadn't. One glance and her heart began to flutter wildly. The control he had over her was both dangerous and foolish. The stranger's words about Cole having a way with women sparked her indignation.

"What does it look like?" she shot back, slamming the blunt edge of the shovel into the compact snow on her driveway. Now, if she could only hold her tongue . . . But sometimes it was impossible to hold things back.

"Let me do that. It's too hard for you."

"It is not too hard for me." Her hand tightened its grip on the wooden handle.

"Don't be silly. I don't want you out here—"

"I'm sure that's true. You'd like to be rid of me all together . . . and it's not because you're attracted to me, either."

His laugh was mirthless. "What's that supposed to mean?"

Lesley swung around, intent on ignoring him.

"What's so important about doing this now? I was planning to do it in the morning. It doesn't make sense to do it twice."

"It makes perfect sense," she shouted, and

tossed a shovel full of snow to the side. "Now kindly leave me alone."

"Lesley, please. Will you listen to reason?"

"Reason?" she echoed. "All these weeks I've watched you. It isn't normal, the way you live. A hundred questions demand answers."

"What are you talking about?"

"It doesn't matter. Go inside where it's safe and you don't have to deal with me."

"Lesley." He sounded exasperated and angry.

By this time she didn't care. "But then I could be easily silenced." She paused and placed a hand on her hip, her chin angled flippantly. "After all, you do have a way with women. I'm no problem." Realizing what she said, Lesley gasped and turned around.

His hand, biting roughly into her upper arm, turned her to face him. "What did you say?"

Pinching her lips tightly shut, she met his angry glare. "Nothing."

"Don't give me that."

"I just did." The acid sting of tears burned in her eyes. How could she possibly have fallen for someone like Cole Daniels?

"Lesley." He ground out her name impatiently.

She could feel the heat of his gaze studying her face, pausing to linger for a heart-stopping moment on her parted mouth.

Lesley struggled. At the first sign of resistance, Cole dropped his hand.

"Don't make judgments when you don't understand the situation." He ran a hand through his hair. His steel-sharp gaze pinned her as effectively as a vise. "What else did you hear?"

With a determined effort, Lesley lowered her eyes. "Enough, Mr. Engstrom." When she glanced up, she saw that Cole had closed his eyes, his mouth tight and controlled.

"Have you told anyone?"

Lesley shook her head. "Are you in any danger?"

"No."

He was lying, Lesley was sure of it. Hadn't the stranger said Jennings was after him?

"Are you in trouble with the authorities?"

"No," he said forcefully.

"Are you going to tell me what's going on?"

"Lesley," he pleaded and rubbed a weary hand over his face. "I can't. I could be putting you . . ." He didn't finish. Instead he took the shovel out of her hand. "Invite me in for coffee."

"All right," she agreed.

Stomping snow off her boots, Lesley led the way into the cozy, warm apartment. Cole followed her inside, sitting at the table while she placed the water on the stove to boil. For a second she stood, unsure, in the middle of her kitchen. She didn't know whether she should remain by the stove and wait for the water or sit beside Cole. Her first instinct was to wrap her arms around him and seek the comfort of his embrace.

Hesitantly Lesley stood with her back to him, her hands gripping the oven door to keep from turning and letting him see the doubts and anxiety in her eyes.

The scraping sound of the chair told Lesley that Cole was standing. The noise was followed by gentle footsteps moving behind her. A rough, calloused hand cupped each shoulder, bringing her back to rest against his solid length. His mouth found the sensitive area behind her ear and spread teasing kisses there. Tingling sensations shot down her back and arms.

"Cole," she moaned, close to tears, "don't, please don't."

He turned her in his arms, and Lesley struggled against surrendering to his stronger, more dominant will. Was she just another woman he was manipulating?

Some of the hurtful skepticism must have shown in her eyes.

"Can you trust me?" Cole questioned softly.

It would be so easy to fall completely captive to the power of his magnetism. She tucked her chin down and a cloud of dark brown curls fell forward, wreathing her face. "I don't know anymore. I don't even know your name and . . . ."

A finger lifted her chin so that their eyes could meet. "It's Daniel Cole Engstrom." Something flickered from his eyes . . . doubt, regret?

Was it a name she should recognize? Lesley

didn't. Her brow was marred with thick lines of concentration. "What should I call you?"

"Friend?" he murmured, then shook his head. "No, what I feel for you goes far beyond a simple friendship." His mouth was drawing closer and closer. "Lover?" he continued. "No, that's something for the future. Our future."

Her heart was pounding against her ribs like a sledgehammer. His hand curved around the side of her neck. His fingers weaved into the dark strands of hair and raised her head a fraction of an inch to meet his descending mouth.

Wave after wave of heat flowed over her. For days she'd longed for the warmth, the feel, the wonder of Cole's arms. His mouth moved over hers again and again, caressing her lips with persuasive mastery. And fool that she was, Lesley was a willing slave. Her arms circled his middle and she pressed herself to him, reveling in the scents of spicy after-shave and hard work.

When he buried his face in the side of her neck, it was all Lesley could do not to weep. Was she so spineless that Cole could wrap her around his finger with nothing more persuasive than a series of kisses?

The teakettle began to whistle, and reluctantly Cole released her, but his hands lingered on her shoulders for an extra moment. His thumb wiped aside a maverick tear and kissed her cheek.

Lesley's hands were shaking when she brought

111

down the mugs. Why did he have to be so gentle? If he had been the least bit rough, she could have resisted him.

"What should I call you?" she asked again, her voice slightly husky as she placed his mug on the table. He still hadn't told her. Was this another game he was playing?

"Cole."

She nodded and sat opposite him. Both hands surrounded the hot mug, burning the sensitive area of her palms. Lesley almost welcomed the pain. Her gaze was centered on the steaming liquid.

"Can you trust me a little longer? Then I'll explain everything."

"And if I can't?"

His hand reached for hers, squeezing it. "I don't know, but I know you, Lesley, and I'm asking you to trust me for just a little while longer."

"Why should I trust you? Give me one good reason," she demanded.

"There isn't one. I know what you must be thinking."

"You couldn't possibly know."

"I didn't want to bring you into any of this."

"Into any of what?" she cried.

She saw that Cole was quickly losing the fragile grip on his patience. His jaw clenched and he expelled a long, impatient breath. "I knew the minute I saw you we were headed for trouble."

Lesley had known it, too.

"When I saw that you were the girl who lived next door, I should have packed my bags and left town. You're far too lovely for my level of concentration. And then when you dressed up for the Halloween party I knew there was no help for me. I might as well—"

"Don't talk to me like that, Cole." Pain seared her heart. She couldn't look at him. The thought that she was only another conquest was more than she could bear. Purposely, she lowered her gaze, but not before she noted the bewildered look in his eyes.

"Talk to you like what?" His voice was devoid of emotion.

It hurt to speak, the tightness in her throat was almost strangling. "I'm not like your other women. I don't want to hear meaningless phrases of love and devotion. Because I don't believe you. I can't. Not when everything you've done has been a lie."

She noticed how his hand gripped the mug. "I've never lied to you."

Lesley released a bitter laughing sigh. "You just did. I heard the man say that someone was after you. Jennings, I think his name was." She flipped her hand over in a gesture of helplessness. "I heard him say you were in danger, and yet when I asked, you denied it."

"I'm perfectly safe here," he answered forcefully. "No one knows where I am. Do you think I'd place you in a situation that could cause you harm? Do you honestly think that of me?" The lack of emotion in his voice made his words all the more profound. "What kind of man do you think I am?"

"I don't know what my opinion of you is anymore," she replied with taunting disdain.

An ominous silence followed. "Then there's nothing more I can say, is there?"

"No, I don't think there is."

Lesley remained sitting when Cole stood, his chair scraping against the linoleum floor. The front door closed softly, but the sound of it echoed across the room in ear-shattering decibels.

Love thy neighbor, love thy neighbor, love thy neighbor. . . . A hundred times during the night the words were repeated in her thoughts.

Sleep eluded her. Never had she been more conscious of the man next door. Only a thin layer of wall separated them, and yet Lesley felt as if they lived on different planets. How could she believe him when he said the words she longed to hear? Everything about Daniel Cole Engstrom was a lie.

About two o'clock Lesley gave up the effort and crawled out of bed. Her Bible sat on the living room end table, and she curled up on the davenport reading through Psalms. Gradually her lashes began to flutter downward and she slept. Her night was spent on the sofa without a pillow.

The crick in her neck was painful when Lesley rose the next morning. Rotating her head seemed to ease the tension somewhat, but not enough for her to avoid favoring it. She dressed more casually than usual, in wool pants and a matching jacket.

The driveway was cleared for her car, and Lesley realized that Cole must have been up early to shovel it for her. The kindness made her love for him all the more potent.

Lesley was halfway to the car when she noticed that Cole was still at work, clearing the area around the mailbox. He turned just as she opened her car door. One dark brow quirked mockingly in her direction.

"Lesley," he began quietly, a serious note running through his tone. He stopped, but Lesley was sure he had wanted to say something more. A veiled look came over his face. "Have a good day."

"Thank you," she returned stiffly. "I will."

She didn't, of course. With so much of Cole dominating her thoughts and time, she made one mistake after another, until the bank manager gave her a peculiar look.

"Are you feeling all right, Lesley?" Ben Fullbright came up to her desk. His look was sincere.

"I may have a touch of the flu," Lesley returned with the hint of a smile.

"Do you feel you'd like to take the rest of the day off?" her employer inquired further.

"No, I'm fine. Thanks." Her hand tightened around the pencil until she was sure it would snap.

"Just say if you feel worse later."

"Thanks." She released a slow, impatient sigh. "I will."

About noon, her nerves stretched taut, Lesley couldn't stand it any longer. She couldn't work. There wasn't a time in her life she'd felt more tired. Her neck ached and she wanted to go home.

Cole stepped out of his apartment the minute she pulled into the driveway. "Are you all right?"

"No."

He appeared to study the troubled, confused light in her eyes, his own look darkening. "What's wrong?"

"What's wrong?" she cried. "I can't even work. Nothing's right! I need answers, and I need them now."

"Lesley." He breathed in deeply as if to control his rising temper. "Trust me, for just a little while longer. Then I'll explain everything."

A protesting sob rose quickly to her throat and she shook her head. "I can't. I just can't."

The phone inside her apartment was ringing and Lesley pivoted sharply.

"Honey, please."

The endearment rolled off his tongue as if he'd said it a hundred times to a hundred different women.

Ignoring him, Lesley squared her shoulders and walked inside her apartment.

"Hello." Her voice was breathless as she spoke into the receiver.

"This is the library," the efficient voice returned. "The bank said I could contact you at this number."

"Yes?" Her heart was pounding at double time.

"We have the information you requested."

Chapter Six

Her purse still clenched in her hand, Lesley flew back out the front door, slamming it after her.

"Where are you going in such an all-fired hurry?" Cole shouted.

Lesley nearly stumbled off the top step, catching herself just in time. She hadn't expected Cole to be outside. "The . . . the library," she supplied on a breathless note.

"Is the place on fire?"

"No." Willing her pounding heart to be still, she opened the car door, climbed inside and started the engine.

"Then wait."

"No! I'm leaving and I'm leaving now."

Cole's look was bewildered, as if he couldn't understand a woman who was demanding answers one moment, then fleeing the next without a logical explanation. Lesley didn't care; he'd left her to face countless unresolved questions.

Although more outwardly calm, her hands were shaking as she gripped the strap of her purse and strolled into the library.

The woman who had helped her earlier was out to lunch but had left the information at the desk for Lesley.

ENGSTROM, DANIEL. His name was followed by a listing of dates and articles that showed Cole had been in the paper, at least *The New York Times*, on several occasions.

Briefly her eyes scanned the dates and articles. Cole was some kind of automobile executive. Although still reading, she walked across the library floor and sat at the table next to the shelves that contained the encyclopedias. Dynamic Engines Corporation kept appearing along with Cole's name. That was in Michigan. What was he doing with an out-of-state check issued from Indiana?

The information was scant at best. Wondering where she should search next, Lesley pulled out the latest edition of the business directory. He wasn't listed there, nor was he in Who's Who in America.

As she was returning the volume, she saw another book labeled Who's Who in Finance and Industry. Her fingers flipped open the pages and ran down the row of *E*'s.

Engstrom, Daniel Cole. Her finger stopped as she sank back into the cushioned chair and continued reading: AUTOMOBILE EXECUTIVE. That she knew. SINGLE. Thank goodness. EDUCATION: Bachelor of Science in industrial engineering at the Lawrence Institute of Technology. Master's in auto science. Degree in mechanical engineering from Chrysler Industries. MBA from the University of Michigan. Hired as an engineer for Dynamic Engines and promoted to the director of advanced engineering and finally chief engineer.

Chief engineer! Lesley propped her head up with one hand pressed tightly across her forehead as the knowledge of his expertise washed over her.

Again she scanned the statistical information. Cole was thirty-four and had accomplishments men twenty years his senior would envy. But why hide himself away like this? For what reason? Should she confront him with what she knew? Or wait until he told her and see if his story jelled with what she'd learned?

Her thoughts muddled, Lesley walked outside the building and headed down the street toward her car.

"Hey, what are you doing shopping this time of day?" Terry pulled her car into the empty parking space beside Lesley's and rolled down her window.

"Oh, hi," Lesley responded with an absent smile.

"Hi yourself. What's up?"

"Up? What makes you think anything's up?"

"In addition to being your sister, I happen to

120

know you, Lesley Joy Brown. Now, out with it."

"Cole Daniels is really Daniel Cole Engstrom," Lesley announced without preamble.

"What?" Terry gasped and jerked open her car door. "I think we need to talk." She unstrapped Lisa from the baby seat in the back of the car.

Fifteen minutes later they sat in their favorite café drinking coffee while Lesley explained what she'd learned from the library.

"I don't believe it."

"That's the tenth time you've said that," Lesley commented with an impatient snap to her voice.

"Sorry."

Lesley could tell Terry wasn't actually sorry. "Shocked" was a better word.

"What are you going to do about it?" Terry continued.

"I don't know. What do you think I should do?"

"Confront him?"

"Should I?"

"I'm asking, not telling." Terry turned her attention to Lisa, who was cheerfully eating a soda cracker, mashing it together with her chubby fingers.

"There are so many unexplainables with this."

"I've got it." Terry hit her hand across the plastic-topped table, directing the attention of half the café to their booth in the corner. "It's only logical."

"What?" Lesley leaned forward eagerly across the table. Nothing about this whole thing was logical.

"We're always reading about automobile recalls."

"So?"

"As chief engineer, wouldn't Cole—"

"Of course," Lesley interrupted. "He found out something that's wrong with the cars that would demand a recall. But D.E. is trying to hide this from the customers and has hired a hit man to do in Cole."

"What do you think?"

"I think we may have stumbled onto something," Lesley answered thoughtfully.

"What can we do?"

"Nothing." Lesley propped her chin on a palm. "We're going to have to trust the Lord with this one." Lesley took a sip from her coffee cup. "Cole keeps telling me that everything will be settled soon. I heard him say he was about to hand over the evidence or report or something."

"What are you going to do until then?"

"Thanksgiving's this week, and the bank's closed for the four-day holiday. I think I'll phone in sick tomorrow and stick around. At least, if anything happens, I'll be there to make sure Cole's all right. Let's hope the whole thing will be cleared up by the weekend."

Terry handed Lisa another cracker. The baby

immediately glommed onto it, stuffing it into her small mouth. "You know, I feel like Nancy Drew all of a sudden—protecting the world from evil and upholding the cause of righteousness."

Lesley tossed her sister a disdainful look. "Honestly, Terry, that was Zorro."

The older sister wrinkled her nose. "Yeah, I guess you're right."

Lesley drove home slowly, wondering how she would react to Cole when she saw him. She was terrible at keeping secrets. Her friends knew her well enough to realize that if they wanted something kept quiet, it was better not to tell Lesley. It wasn't that she was a gossip, but anything that was meant to be kept to herself had a way of rolling off her tongue. Already, although she had the best intentions, she'd blurted out what she'd overheard.

The first thing she did when she walked into her apartment was phone the bank and tell Ben Fullbright that she wouldn't be in for the remainder of the week. Slight feelings of guilt invaded her resolve as she replaced the telephone receiver. The day before Thanksgiving was always busy at the bank, but she had to stick close to home for Cole's sake. She smiled, envisioning his reaction if he knew that she was calling in sick in order to stay at the apartment and protect him.

The light tapping sound on the other side of her

wall reminded her of a high school drum cheer. She walked across the room and returned with her own message.

A moment later her doorbell rang. It was Cole.

"Hi." Her eyes avoided his.

"I've been waiting to talk to you."

"Oh?"

"Are you suddenly reduced to responses of one syllable?" He regarded her skeptically.

"No." Her eyes followed the worn pattern in the carpet.

Cole's index finger under her chin lifted her gaze to his. "I think we'd better talk?"

"Do you want coffee or Iacocca . . . I mean cocoa." She turned and hurried into the kitchen. Oh no! She'd nearly done it again.

Cole followed her, a hand on her shoulder stopping her as she held the teakettle under the faucet. "What'd you say?"

"Nothing." She prayed he wouldn't question her further.

"Something about Iacocca?"

"No, silly," she said, desperately trying to brush off her blunder. "Cocoa, as in heated chocolate milk with melted marshmallows."

"All right, I'll have the Iacocca."

"The what?" She looked up, startled.

"All right, Lesley." Cole's hands gripped her shoulders and turned her around. "Are you going to say it, or am I?"

She felt like stamping her foot and groaning her frustration with herself. "I didn't want you to know that I'd learned."

"Exactly what do you know?"

"About the recall and everything."

"The recall?" His look was completely blank. "I think we'd better sit down and get this into the open." He took the kettle out of her hand and set it aside.

Lesley turned off the burner and followed him into the living room.

"Sit," he instructed, and gently settled her into the winged back chair that was positioned in the corner by the front windows.

Cole paced in front of her. Lesley's neck hurt to look up at him, but she wanted to watch his face, study the emotion that came from the dark, fathomless eyes. With a hand at the base of her neck she rubbed some of the tension from the muscles along the back of the sensitive area.

"What's wrong?" Cole looked down as if noticing her actions for the first time.

"I slept on the sofa last night without a pillow, and now my neck's killing me."

"Here, let me rub it for you," he offered and walked around behind the chair. His hands felt warm against her skin, and soon a tingling heat was spreading over her. Lesley closed her eyes to the potency of his touch. Her bones seemed to melt as his fingers gently kneaded the area.

"How does that feel?"

Was she hearing things, or did his husky voice sound as disturbed as she was feeling?

"Wonderful." The one word managed to make it past the sluggishness that affected her throat muscles. Feelings of languor, a tender dreamy state, took over her mind. "Oh, Cole," she murmured softly.

"Crazy woman, what were you doing on the sofa? You should have been in bed."

"I know." His gentle, massaging hands continued the slow rotating movements that eased the coiled tension from her. "But I couldn't sleep."

"Because of me?" The question was issued softly, in coaxing tones.

"Yes," she moaned softly. "Do we have to talk? Can't you just let your fingers work their magic?"

His soft chuckle caused her eyes to flutter open. "Did I just say something I shouldn't have again?"

"Again?" he prompted.

"I do that, you know."

His hands kneaded her shoulders, his thumbs finding the spot between her shoulder blades. "Yes, that's one thing I've noticed these last weeks."

It seemed important that she gather her resolve. Slowly she straightened, yearning for his touch, yet actively breaking contact. "I . . . it feels fine now. Thanks."

Cole moved around the chair and sat on the edge of the living room sofa. "You'd better explain what you know."

Lesley folded her hands together in her lap, as if laced fingers would lend her the strength to speak freely. "I found your name at the library today." He shrugged as if her knowing that didn't trouble him. "You're an important man, Cole Engstrom."

"But stupid." His eyes hardened and he seemed to look straight through her.

"Stupid?" she repeated.

Cole leaned forward and joined his hands. "Incredibly so."

"Is that why you're hiding?" Why couldn't he just come right out and explain? Was she going to have to pry every bit of information out of him?

That hard, chiseled look came over his face again, and he stared at her stonily.

"Cole?" she prompted.

Lightly he shook himself. "It's not what you think."

"There is no recall?"

A poor replica of a smile briefly touched his troubled features. "Honey, if you had any idea how carefully each car, each model, is investigated before ever hitting a showroom floor you wouldn't even suggest it. D.E. is proud of its record, and with good reason."

"But . . ."

"Lesley." He said her name in a sober breath. "Will you go out to dinner with me tonight?"

Lesley opened and closed her mouth, then nodded eagerly. "Is it safe for you to be seen?"

That intense look came over him. "Safe enough, but if I stay in that apartment another minute I'll go mad." He smiled then, one of those rare earth-shattering, wonderful smiles that would disarm even the most hardhearted. "But then, the reason for my insanity could be attributed to my lovely neighbor."

"That's unfair, I've been more than—" Lesley stopped. How easily she fell prey to this man's games!

His eyes glinted with mischief as Lesley gave him a bemused smile.

"You like doing that, don't you?" she accused, feigning anger.

"It's easy to get a reaction out of you."

The words had a strange effect on her. Her reaction, as he called it, had a lot to do with her feelings for him.

"You ready?" Cole stood and extended a hand to her.

Lesley glanced at her wristwatch. "It's barely three."

"I know. I wanted to avoid the dinner crowd."

"You'll give me some answers?"

Cole met her narrowed gaze and nodded thoughtfully. "If you insist."

"I do," she said more forcefully than she meant to. Why did it seem that after every meeting she was left with more questions than when she started? But not this time, she vowed.

They drove to Post Falls, a small community to the west of Coeur d'Alene, and ate at a restaurant that overlooked the Spokane River.

"Tell me about Coeur d'Alene?" Cole asked after the waitress had taken their order. Apparently Cole was hungry, since he asked for the largest steak in the house. Lesley's own appetite was more modest, and she ordered salmon.

"Well," she said with a smile, "it's the largest city in the northern panhandle of Idaho and the county seat of Kootenai County."

"Kootenai County?"

"Yes. Try saying that three times without a breath." Her hand slipped around the chilled water glass. Lesley loved Idaho. She felt as if she'd been born and raised in some of the most beautiful country on God's earth.

"I love the lake," she continued softly. "It's been said that Coeur d'Alene Lake is one of the ten most beautiful lakes in the world. It has a hundred miles of forested shoreline with nature trails and scenic walks. This is God's country, Cole Daniels." She stopped, her eyes narrowing with frustration, when she realized what she'd said.

"Engstrom," Cole corrected.

"Yes," she mumbled and lowered her eyes to the white tablecloth. "I keep forgetting." He'd done it again. She had come expecting him to explain some of the things that had been happening, and he had quickly manipulated her into doing all the talking.

Cole chuckled, apparently noticing that she was on to his game. "I wish you could see your eyes. I can't recall seeing anything more expressive."

"Oh no you don't."

"Don't?"

"Change the subject again." Cole was clever. She'd say that for him. "Cole, don't do this to me, please." The last words were issued in a soft pleading tone that spoke of weeks of uncertainty.

"Can you trust me just a little while longer? Within the week everything will be out in the open," Cole said tightly.

"I think it's a matter of faith all right, but of your trusting me."

"I got into this mess because I depended on someone else." The hard, masculine line of his mouth narrowed. "I won't be taken in so easily again."

"I'm not trying to take you in." Nervously her tongue moistened her lower lip. What kind of person did Cole think she was? "Do you think I'll run to the press? Is that it?"

"You could." The cynicism, the bitterness from whatever was happening to him vibrated in his words.

Hurt rippled through her. The pain of its aftermath brought stinging tears to the back of her eyes. With a determined effort, Lesley was able to forestall their flow. "I don't suppose you realize that the mining district just east of the city is still one of the largest lead-, zinc- and silver-producing areas in the world. Also, the Powderhouse Museum that was part of the original Fort Sherman is located at North Idaho College." She continued to ramble until her voice cracked. She inhaled a quivering breath and bowed her head.

"Lesley." Her name came on a low, pleading breath.

"It's all right," she said shakily. "Really. I understand. If it's trust you want, you've got mine. You may not have been around long, but I know one thing—you're not a criminal, Cole. I'll wait because that's what you want and seem to need from me."

A smile trembled from her lips when she raised her eyes to meet his. His gaze was glistening, his expression brooding and thoughtful, but he said nothing and she didn't either. Their meal arrived and they ate in silence.

Cole's knife sliced across the rare T-bone steak. "Do you know much about air bags?"

The question came so casually that Lesley didn't catch the importance.

"You mean the ones airlines hand out?"

"No," Cole mocked her softly. "I mean the ones in cars. Those little toys I tinker around with."

"Oh." Lesley took a sip of her coffee. "No, I can't say that I do."

"It's been estimated that air bags installed in automobiles could save up to two thousand lives every year."

"Why don't car makers install them, then?" Lesley hoped to appear as nonchalant as possible. She didn't know what Cole was telling her, but it obviously had great importance to him.

"Only Mercedes-Benz offers this safety measure as an option on their automobiles, but at the cost of eight hundred dollars it's an expensive option."

"Yes." Lesley swallowed. "Yes, it is."

"It would mean quite a bit to highway safety if these devices could be made and installed cheaply in American cars, wouldn't it?"

"Two thousand lives." She quoted his own figures back to him.

Cole laid his knife across the top of the plate and pushed his chair back. His hand rested across his stomach. "That was one terrific steak."

"Mine too," Lesley echoed. Cole was kind enough not to comment that she had barely touched her meal.

He paid their tab and left a generous tip. His hand possessively cupped her elbow as he led the way out of the restaurant and into his car. He held the car door open for her, and his eyes rested on the dashboard momentarily, then flickered to her in an apologetic smile.

"I've only figured out the driver's side." He spoke absently. He closed her door and, puzzled, Lesley watched as he stared into space for a moment. The skies were obliterated. There wasn't a star in the heavens. Even the moon was invisible, tucked behind a thick layer of clouds. Still she glanced upward, wondering what Cole found so fascinating.

He climbed into his side of the car and started the engine. Placing his hand along the back of the seat, he looked behind him, prepared to back out of the parking space. As he turned his head, their eyes met and held for a breathless second.

"You're an incredibly beautiful woman, Lesley Brown."

Lesley's gaze darted downward. Was this one of his lines meant to disarm her? If so, he had succeeded beyond even her expectations. "Thank you," she mumbled.

A finger lightly traced her chin and, following the delicate line of her face, traveled over her ear and down the side of her neck. The long, male finger entwined with the dark curls at the base of her neck. The gentle pressure brought her mouth within inches of his.

He bent forward and brushed his lips against the sensitive skin at the hollow of her neck. Lesley turned her head, thrilling to the delicious shivers that skidded over her skin.

His warm breath fanned her face. "Just a little while longer, I promise, Lesley," he murmured deeply. The searing kiss that followed his words stole her breath away as it sealed his promise.

One hand continued to keep her close to his side as he leisurely made the return trip to the duplex. Lesley directed him down country roads and teasingly pointed out local landmarks.

When Cole pulled into the driveway, Lesley felt an eerie sensation run over her.

"Cole," she said and was shocked at the sound of her own voice. It was weak and uneven, yet brittle. "Something's wrong."

He was instantly alert, his cat eyes taking in the area with one sweeping glare. "Someone's broken into my apartment," he announced and pushed open his car door.

Chapter Seven

"No," Lesley cried and lunged for Cole's arm. She'd do anything to stop him from going inside the apartment. "You can't go in there. They could be waiting."

Cole didn't seem to hear her. He brushed her hand aside as if her grip were no more effective than a child's.

"Cole," she pleaded a second time.

He had apparently forgotten her presence until Lesley climbed out his side of the car and ran after him. With all her weight she pulled against his arm. "Cole," she cried frantically. "You could be killed."

He turned to her then, his eyes shining with an unnatural light. Hate. Never had Lesley seen anything more vivid in a man's eyes. Cole hated with an intensity that paled under every other emotion. His reactions were single-minded— even common sense was banished under the all-consuming drive.

Realizing nothing could effectively stop him, Lesley flung herself in front of Cole. His hands tried to push her behind him, but she clung to him, her own fear giving her strength beyond her normal capabilities.

"Lesley," Cole groaned and gripped her around the waist, holding her upright. His face muscles had relaxed and the intensity had waned. "If anyone was in there waiting, they could have killed us both several times over."

"Oh." She swallowed, and loosened her hold.

"You put your life on the line for me." His face loomed bare inches from her own. "Why?"

"I . . . I didn't want to see you hurt." Her love had driven her just as his hate had him. But she couldn't tell him that, she couldn't give him another weapon.

Cole raked a hand through the dark hair that swept naturally over his forehead. "You can be the most exasperating female."

"Me?" she shouted incredulously.

He ignored her outrage and folded her fingers in his. "Come on, let's go see what damage they've done."

"Who?" Lesley wanted to know. "Jennings?"

Lesley felt the tremor that went through Cole as he tensed and glanced down at her. "No, that isn't his style. Jennings has others do his dirty work for him."

Cole pushed open the door to his apartment with one hand. It banged against the wall, and the sound vibrated through the room. One flip of the light switch and the area was flooded with light.

Lesley let out a sickened gasp at the mess that lay before her. The living room was in shambles, the furniture slashed and the stuffing pulled from the cushions. Something had been thrown through the television screen and the shattered glass was everywhere. Her gaze followed the path of destruction through the apartment.

Speechless with shock, they moved into the kitchen. The contents of the refrigerator had been dumped on the floor. Egg yolks and milk jelled on the linoleum. A bag of flour had been carelessly tossed across the top of the counter and stove.

"Oh, Cole." Lesley could hardly bear to look. In all her life she had never seen worse chaos. "We'd better phone the police."

"No!" he shouted.

"Yes," she returned stubbornly. "You can't let this kind of destruction go unreported."

"I know who did this and I know why. The police won't help."

"But, Cole," she argued.

"I thought you said you could trust me?" He made the shouting words a question. "Women are like that, aren't they? They say one thing when they mean another. Is that something ingrained in you from youth?"

Lesley stared back at him dumbfounded, unable to answer.

"Why should I tell you anything? What right do you have to invade my life and demand answers to questions that are none of your business?"

"None," she answered in a soft, trembling voice. "None whatsoever."

Cole rammed both hands into his jeans pockets and shot a gaze at the ceiling. Neither spoke for several long moments.

"They didn't find what they were looking for. That's the reason for this." His hand made a sweeping gesture toward the kitchen and living room.

Lesley nodded, realizing that in his own way he was apologizing for his outburst. He was angry and lashing out at her. His reaction hurt, but it was understandable.

Avoiding as much of the egg and milk as possible, Lesley walked across the kitchen and took the broom from the narrow closet on the other side of the refrigerator.

"What are you doing?" he asked with a confused look.

"Cleaning up. It's got to be done." And if she was occupied, it would be easier to swallow back the questions that demanded answers. Who had done this? Why? And what were they searching for so desperately?

"Lesley," Cole groaned and took the broom out of her hand. "I'll do that. I don't want you to have to deal with this mess."

"But I want to help." Her voice wobbled treacherously. "You're always pushing me away —let me at least do this."

He didn't look pleased about it, but he managed a grin. "Any other woman in the world would have stormed off, and with good reason. I didn't mean to shout at you."

"I know," she supplied softly. "But I understand."

An unreadable expression passed over his face. His eyes seemed to caress her. Lesley swallowed tightly. The anguish, the mental torment he was enduring, was all there for her to read. Every part of her yearned to reach out and comfort him.

"Do what you can in there and I'll tackle the living room." Cole broke eye contact first, pivoting sharply into the other room. Lesley watched him for a few moments as he stooped over to pick up the glass, but soon concentrated on her own efforts.

"If we were still hungry, I might have been able to cook something out of this," she teased.

Cole made a disgusted sound and continued working.

With a soft smile lighting up her eyes, Lesley decided to dump the flour mess on the counter onto the floor before tackling that. With the broom she swept it off the counter. The white powdery substance filled the air until it was almost impossible to see. She coughed and waved her hand in front of her face. When the air cleared she glanced up to find Cole standing, hands on hips, watching her, his eyes filled with amusement.

Lesley brushed the hair from her eyes. Her hand came away caked with the fine dusting of flour.

"Here, let me do that," Cole muttered and took a step toward her.

"Don't you dare," she cautioned. "You'll track the flour everywhere."

"You come here, then." He pointed to the place where the carpet ended, where the living room met the kitchen.

Lesley did as he requested, attempting to brush the flour from her face and hair.

Cole sighed audibly. "You're only making it worse." He took a handkerchief from his hip pocket and made a show of unfolding it.

"That had better be clean," Lesley admonished with laughing eyes.

He laughed as he brushed the hair from her cheek and lightly ran the soft cotton cloth over her face. Although his touch was cool and impersonal, Lesley's reaction was overwhelming. Her teeth bit into her bottom lip. Immediately she regretted the telltale action and forced a bright smile onto her taut mouth.

"Thanks." She cast her gaze downward.

"Lesley." Her name was murmured in a soft tone, and when she glanced up she watched, amazed, as a nerve flexed tensely in his jaw. Her heart leaped at the tender look in his eyes.

Smiling gently, Lesley reached up and caressed his cheek, her hand lovingly stroking the proud line of his jaw. Cole's hand covered hers and directed it to his lips. Lightly he kissed her palm. The teasing gesture made her knees grow weak, and she locked her arms around his neck and fit her body to his.

Cole wrapped his arms around her and covered her mouth with hungry kisses that skyrocketed her to dizzying heights. The first taste of longing raced through her blood, catching her unaware. Frightened and more than a little unsure, she released her hold and levered herself away.

Cole relaxed his grip and expelled a long, shuddering breath. His eyes were still closed.

"I . . . I got flour on you," Lesley managed after a moment, her voice unsteady. Gently she brushed it from his shirt. Her palm could feel the rapid beat of Cole's heart and the labored breathing as he struggled for control.

"I'll get back to work," Lesley said and was surprised at the sound of her own voice. It was scratchy and weak.

Silently they worked in different rooms, at their separate tasks, but they were together mentally, even spiritually, in a way Lesley found unexplainable. She remembered stories her mother had told her as a child about the years

Lesley's father was in the war. Months on end, and there was no word, no letters. Her mother didn't know if he was dead or alive, and yet somehow she did know, because the love they had for each other ran so deep that it spanned time and distance. At the time Lesley hadn't understood and must have looked puzzled. When you love, her mother had explained, then you'll know. Years later, Lesley discovered the same sensation for this mysterious man, working silently in the room next to hers. But they could have been continents apart and it wouldn't have mattered.

"You look very intense."

Cole's comment caught her off guard. "I was just thinking," she answered without meeting his eyes. The floor had been cleaned and mopped, the counters scrubbed. The transformation in the small kitchen was dramatic, as was the contrast in the living room where Cole was working.

"What will you do about the furniture? Almost everything will need to be replaced."

"I'm not sure it would be worth the trouble," Cole answered her thoughtfully. "I won't be around here much longer."

The rest of what he was saying faded into oblivion. Wouldn't be around here much longer, Lesley's mind echoed. He was leaving, within a matter of days. He'd pack his bags and without a backward glance be on his way. She meant nothing: a small-town girl who was a convenient distraction. Cole would leave without a thought, without looking back, and with him would go her heart. How could she have been so stupid as to fall in love with this man? Didn't she recognize in the library that a man like Cole wouldn't want anything to do with a nobody like her?

Lesley felt the shock vibrate through her. "Where will you go?" The question was squeezed out through the tight block of pain that formed in her throat.

"More questions?" His look seemed to sear right to her heart. Fresh pain washed through her.

For a moment Lesley stared at him blankly. She felt the blood drain from her face, her breath caught in her lungs, but she answered him with a short shake of her head. "No," she managed. Her hand was shaking visibly as she replaced the broom and mop in the narrow closet. She made a show of looking at her watch, but couldn't have guessed at the time.

"It's getting late. I'll say good night." Her eyes refused to meet his.

His hand on her shoulder stopped her as she stepped into the living room. His touch sent shock waves rippling over her skin. She shrugged her shoulder, breaking the contact. "Don't," she warned in a wavering voice. "Don't touch me." Each word was enunciated plainly so there would be no doubt about her feelings.

"You're angry." Cole sounded surprised.

"You know, sometimes your brilliant perceptions astonish even me," she returned flippantly. "Good night, Cole."

He looked so shocked that she almost wanted to laugh. With her head held high and her chin angled regally, Lesley marched past him. The short distance that separated their front doors was covered in a matter of seconds.

Lesley opened her front door, looked up and let out a bloodcurdling scream.

Chapter Eight

"Lesley." Cole shot into the apartment, nearly knocking her off her feet as he pulled her into his arms.

He stopped abruptly and looked around at the horrible mess that lay scattered before them. "How could they do this?" he muttered in a low, disbelieving voice.

The room was in shambles. Furniture was overturned. Photos of family and friends had been hurled across the room. Drawers were emptied and their contents spilled onto the floor. Lesley felt like screaming and weeping all at the same moment. But the only sound that came from her throat was an anguished cry like that of an animal caught in a hunter's trap. Her life lay sprawled before her. She felt vulnerable, as if she'd been violated.

Cole turned her into his arms, his hand at the back of her head holding it against the muscular cushion of his chest. "I'm so sorry," he murmured over and over again. "I never dreamed they'd do this to you."

Lesley welcomed the comfort offered in his embrace. It helped lessen the shock.

"Here." Cole cleared a path for her and righted the chair before sitting her down. "Let me get you something to drink."

Numbly Lesley shook her head. "No, I'm fine." This was a nightmare, some horrible dream that would vanish in the morning. She closed and opened her eyes, hoping the scene would miraculously disappear. But reality faced her. She couldn't sit idle while her home lay in shambles. Yet as hard as she tried to force herself to stand, she couldn't.

Cole was kneeling at her side, his look troubled and tender. "Are you all right?" He smoothed the hair back from her temple. "You're so pale."

"I'm fine," she murmured and brushed his restraining hands aside as she stood with trembling resolve. The first thing she picked up was the small Bible she used for devotions. Checking the inside flap, she noted that the contents had been undisturbed. It was ironic, since it seemed everything else had been destroyed.

The destruction in her half of the duplex wasn't nearly as extensive as in Cole's. It looked as if someone had come through her quarters searching for something. Drawers were opened and left dangling after their contents had been carelessly tossed aside. The scene was the same in the kitchen, bedroom and bathroom.

Cole set the furniture upright and bent over to pick up the broken pieces of glass that had once been her lamp.

Wordlessly Lesley wandered from room to room, surveying the extent of the damage. Hot color invaded her face at the thought of someone entering her bedroom and sorting through her personal items. With practiced care she carefully folded each piece and returned it to her drawers. Next she straightened the mattress on her bed and pulled back the covers and bedspread. The contents of her closet had been tossed on the floor. After examining each dress, blouse and skirt for damage, she replaced them one by one.

When she returned to the living room, Cole had finished cleaning as best he could and glanced up guiltily.

"Don't look at me like that," he said with a tight, pinched look about his handsome face. "Scream, yell, do whatever will make you feel better."

Lesley lowered her eyes and shook her head. What good would screaming do now?

The teakettle whistled, its shrillness piercing the heavy silence that filled the room. Without a word she moved into the kitchen and took the kettle off the burner. The whistle petered out to a soft whine.

Her hands shaking, Lesley brought down the

instant coffee. She poured the boiling water into ceramic mugs and added sugar. Normally she didn't use the sweetener, but she felt she needed it now.

Cole accepted the cup from her and sat at the opposite side of the room watching her. A muscle worked in his jaw while his eyes were more narrowed and determined than she could ever remember seeing them.

"I want you to know I'll pay for everything."

Lesley looked up at him blankly. "Why?" she asked in a breathless voice that sounded strange even to her own ears. "You didn't do this."

"No." His fingers tightened around the handle of the mug. "But it's my fault. None of this would have happened if it hadn't been for me."

"I don't blame you." Lesley didn't know how she could be so calm, but she was amazingly so. She took a sip of the steaming liquid, and when she looked at Cole she was again jarred by the hate that seemed to exude from him.

"It might be a good idea if you moved in with your sister until after the holiday," Cole said, the words brittle.

"No," she answered forcefully. "I'm staying here. This is my home, and I'm not about to let a bunch of hoodlums dictate my life."

"These men play for keeps, Lesley. This isn't the time to stand on principle."

"I don't care," she shot back hotly.

"Honey, I know how you feel."

"You know how I feel?" She echoed his words in a low, taunting voice and laughed sarcastically. "If you knew how I felt you'd be screaming. You ask me to trust you. This isn't any of my business. But you made it mine the minute you moved next door. You could be anyone, or anything, but I don't have the right to question you. Now"— she inhaled a deep breath—"now you want to send me away? Is it for my own safety or because you're afraid of what I'll do once I discover why you're hiding?"

Cole set his mug aside and stood. Lesley watched him as he strode back and forth across the floor. Pacing was something he'd done a lot in recent months. Lesley knew: she'd heard him.

"You know I'm an engineer," he said without looking at her.

"Yes."

"For years the idea of finding an effective and affordable method of manufacturing air bags has nagged at the back of my mind. I spent two difficult years of my life trying to come up with an idea that would work. Six months ago I did it."

"That's wonderful, Cole." He didn't look as if he was pleased with his discovery.

He offered her a strange smile. "It's simple, really. The air bag fits into the car's steering wheel and is programmed so that at the moment of impact—" He stopped. "That's neither here or there. You get the picture."

Lesley did and thought the idea was amazingly simple. "How soon will it be available in cars?"

"That depends. The patent is pending now. Two patents." The words were heavy and dark. He turned to glance at her then, and the tormented look was in his eyes again. "Two patents from two different men, both claiming to have come up with the identical idea."

Lesley didn't need to hear the other man's name. "It's Jennings, isn't it?"

Thoughtfully Cole nodded, his brow marred by thick, creasing lines. "Yes, Jennings."

"But how?"

"Jennings was a friend. He knew about my idea, and once I got the prototype working and the bugs out of the system I showed him. I was enthusiastic." He paused and wiped a hand over his face. "No, stupid," he corrected. "Jennings was smart, I'll say that for him. He waited until I'd figured a way to produce the air bags before taking everything. But I trusted him. We'd worked together for years, and I considered him a friend. He'd been having financial problems, but I never would have guessed he'd stoop this low. He stole my work and two years of my life."

"But surely you can prove it was you."

"It's not that easy," Cole ground out and clenched his hands together. "Jennings took all my papers and my notes. I've reconstructed everything as best I can, but as it stands now, it's my word against his."

"What about the man who came here? What's he got to do with this?"

"That's Peter Lansky."

"Friend?"

"I have no friends," Cole returned forcefully. Lesley wondered how he thought of her, but didn't voice her question.

"Lansky's my attorney," Cole supplied. "It was his idea to have me go into hiding until I could reproduce the evidence that would prove I was the inventor."

"But the check you came into the bank with was issued from Indiana."

"That was another of Lansky's ideas. He insisted I use the phony name and had the funds available from Indiana as a precautionary method."

"Against Jennings," Lesley muttered to herself.

"Right."

"But Jennings knows you're here today is any indication."

"He knows," Cole reiterated.

"Then why didn't he . . ."

"Finish me off?" Cole completed the horrible thought for her. "I don't know. There was ample opportunity."

"They were looking for the report or whatever it was you gave Lansky?"

"It's the only thing they could be after, with one exception."

"What?" Lesley asked with a puzzled frown.

Cole straightened, his demeanor distant. "Me."

Lesley bit into the soft flesh in her inner cheek to keep from crying out. She couldn't bear to lose Cole. If Jennings were to hurt Cole, a part of herself would shrivel up and die with him.

"Now do you understand why it's so important for you to leave? It won't be long, I promise."

"Cole," she pleaded. "I don't want to go. You know I'd go crazy every minute of every day wondering what was happening to you."

"This isn't your battle," he returned forcefully.

"But I'm making it mine. We're in this together," she argued with him on a breathless note. If it wasn't safe here, they could leave, find someplace that was.

"Lesley." He came to kneel in front of her, taking her soft hands in his and raising them to his mouth. "Thank you. But I can't put you in any danger."

"But I'll be with you."

"That's the worst place you could be."

"I'll go crazy not knowing—"

"Only until after Thanksgiving. If I haven't heard anything by then, you can come back." He was coaxing and gentle, and Lesley doubted that there was anything she could refuse him.

"I don't like this."

"I know you don't, and to be honest, I'm not that excited about it either. There's a certain amount of comfort having you around."

"It's my four karate lessons, right?"

"Right," he chuckled, and kissed her briefly on her cheek. "Come on, I'll help you pack."

Lesley pulled the suitcase out from her closet. Ironically, it was one she had replaced only a half hour earlier. Cole sat on the foot of her bed as she filled the small case.

"I'm only taking enough clothes for two days."

"That should be enough time."

"Good." She snapped closed the lid of the small case. "Can I tell Terry why I'm suddenly descending on her doorstep?" At Cole's hesitation, Lesley added, "Give my sister some credit—she's bound to be suspicious if I show up with a bag in my hand."

"All right," Cole agreed, "fill her in, but only briefly. I don't want this out, you can understand that."

"Yes." She nodded, her head adding emphasis to her words. "Yes, I do."

They walked into the living room, and Cole helped her on with her coat, his hand lingering longer than necessary on her shoulders, bringing her close to him for a timeless moment. When he broke the contact, it was Lesley who opened her eyes and expelled a long, quivering sigh.

"I want you to have something," she said.

Cole watched her with a blank look as she moved into the kitchen and took the broom out of the narrow closet. "It worked great on Dale and Larry."

Cole laughed as he accepted the weapon, gripping the handle tightly. "Here." He handed her a slip of paper with a number written boldly across it. "Call me if anything suspicious happens, even if you're not sure."

Mesmerized, Lesley stared at the figures. She had lived next door to Cole all these months and not known his phone number. "Okay."

"Let's go."

"Us?"

"Yes, I want to follow you into town. Jennings' men could still be out there."

A cold shiver of apprehension ran up her spine, and some of the anxiety must have shown in her face.

"Don't worry, it's only a precaution. I don't think they're still around, but I want to be certain. I'm not going to let anything happen to you."

After locking the front door, Cole placed the suitcase in the backseat of her car. Their eyes met when he straightened: his look intense, worried, hers fearful and unsure.

"Honey"—his voice was a husky murmur—"don't look at me like that. It's difficult enough to let you go."

She nodded, tears filling her eyes until Cole swam in and out of her vision.

He kissed her gently and held her close as if sending her away was the hardest thing he had ever done. "I'll be fine, don't worry about me."

"But I will every second."

"I know."

"I'll be praying, too."

"I could use a few prayers. If there's a God in heaven, I'll be awarded the patent."

If! Lesley's mind shouted back. *If!* She wanted to talk to him, explain. But now wasn't the time.

"I'll follow you as far as your sister's."

Lesley agreed with a feeble smile. She climbed into her car and started the engine. Cole followed her into town, waving a brief farewell as she turned into Terry's driveway.

"I can't believe it," Terry muttered, slowly shaking her head back and forth. They sat at the kitchen table, while Lisa was on the floor banging on a set of old pans with a wooden spoon.

"Why do I get the impression that this is a repeat of a previous conversation?"

"I can't help it." Terry shot back a half-angry glare. "It isn't every day I hear this kind of stuff. What did Jennings' men do to your apartment?"

"Dumped things mostly. They were looking for Cole's report, and since they couldn't find it at his house, they must have assumed he'd given it to me. Most of the mess is cleaned up," she answered absently.

"Are you thinking of going to the police?"

"I don't know. I'm not sure what to do. Cole could be in terrible danger, but he definitely wants the police out of it."

"Can you blame him?"

"Yes," she returned loudly. "No," she finished weakly.

"It sounds to me like you're as confused as I am about this whole thing."

"For once, sister dear, we're in agreement."

"How much longer before Cole knows about the patent?"

"Apparently the judge hearing the case is making his decision soon."

"Shouldn't Cole be there?"

"Where?" Lesley looked up blankly.

"At the courthouse, wherever his case is being heard."

"Oh." Lesley took in a deep breath. "I guess not. His attorney seemed to think it would only place him in greater danger. Jennings would have open range on Cole if he'd stayed in Michigan."

"Is that so different from now? If this Jennings character knows that Cole's in Coeur d'Alene, isn't he in even greater danger?"

Lesley's finger made nervous circles around the edge of her coffee cup. "I don't think so. Oh,

Terry, I'm really worried. My life has always been so peaceful and quiet. Who would ever have dreamed all this could happen?"

"Believe me, the next time you start complaining about something mysterious going on at your place I won't question or doubt or anything."

"That's encouraging," Lesley responded with a small, slightly high-pitched laugh.

Lisa banged loudly on an aluminum pan with her wooden spoon, causing both sisters to stop and smile. How safe and secure the baby's life was, compared to the harsh realities of what she was facing with Cole, Lesley mused.

"Lisa's making a joyful noise unto the Lord," Terry teased.

Lesley gazed lovingly at the baby.

The phone rang and Terry rose to answer it. "Hello. Yes, just a minute, she's here." She handed the receiver to Lesley. "It's Cole."

"Oh." Lesley hurried out of her chair. "Cole?" Her voice was thick with anticipation.

"I probably shouldn't have phoned, but I needed to hear your voice after all these weeks of living next to you."

"And complaining about all the noise I made," she added with a happy sigh.

"I'm finding it's incredibly quiet here. Too quiet."

"Don't say that." Lesley tensed, her hand gripping the telephone until she was sure her fingers had made permanent indentations in the hard plastic.

"Not to worry, it's not that kind of quiet. I'm finding that I miss your singing."

"But I can't carry a tune."

"You don't need to tell me that. I know, I've listened to you often enough."

Lesley laughed softly. "You must really be missing me, then."

"That just goes to show you how much."

They spoke for a few minutes longer. Cole's words were reassuring. Much of the terrible tension that had knotted Lesley's stomach all day lessened.

That evening the church was filled almost to capacity. The Wednesday before Thanksgiving was a time the congregation set aside to thank God for His continued blessings throughout the year.

Even after the church had emptied, Lesley sat in the pew, her gaze resting on the huge cross behind the altar. Her mind was filled with prayers for Cole. Mentally she pictured an army of angels surrounding him, offering him spiritual protection. His words "If there's a God" had shocked her. Until that time she wasn't certain where he stood with the Lord. The bitterness and hatred she had witnessed in him from their first confrontation was even more pronounced now. Paul Walker, with his spiritual insight, had sensed Cole's inner struggles at their first meeting.

For her peace of mind, Lesley rushed to the phone as soon as she returned to her sister's house, and dialed the phone number Cole had given her. She let it ring twelve times without an answer. With taut nerves, she hung up and dialed again: still no response. A flood of horrible, heart-stopping fear washed over her. Jennings' men had found Cole! He was hurt. He could be dying. She had to get to him.

Blindly she grabbed her coat and stumbled out of the kitchen.

"What is it?" Terry demanded, noting the pale, bloodless look on Lesley's face.

"Cole," she muttered, feeling numb. "He doesn't answer the phone."

"Les." Terry placed a restraining hand on Lesley's sleeve. "What are you going to do?"

"Go out there and find out if he's all right."

"Les, you can't."

Two pair of intense blue eyes clashed. "I've got to."

"At least wait until Robert gets home. Let him go with you."

"No."

"The Thanksgiving baskets will be delivered soon, he'll be back any minute." There was a desperate ring to Terry's voice.

"And he could be hours. For Cole's sake I've got to go now."

"Maybe we should phone the police?"

"No, that would be premature. Cole could be in the shower or outside or sleeping and not hear the phone. But I've got to be assured he's all right. I'll phone you the minute I know."

Indecision played across Terry's face. "I'll pray," she added. "And if I don't hear from you within forty minutes, I'm calling out the National Guard."

Lesley hardly heard her sister's words, she was so intent on getting to Cole as quickly as possible.

The car headlights illuminated the way as Lesley drove up the hill that led to the duplex. She pulled into the driveway and purposely left the car lights on, flooding the area with beams of light. Both sides of the apartment were dark. Only an hour earlier, Lesley had been sitting in a quiet, peaceful church, praying. Now she stood alone in a dark moonless night, facing . . . she didn't know what.

"Cole?" She cried out his name and waited.

Nothing.

"Cole, answer me."

"Lesley, is that you?"

Relief weakened her knees.

"You idiot, what are you doing here?" Cole questioned as he came around from the back of the house.

She ran to him and threw her arms around his neck, laughing to keep from crying. "I tried to phone and there wasn't an answer. I was frantic! Where were you?"

"In the back, breaking up hay for the deer."

"Why now?"

"It's dark, I figured it was safer at night. I'm not really into this cloak-and-dagger stuff, but it made more sense not to be a target in broad daylight."

"You crazy fool. . . . I didn't know what to think. Let me use your phone. Terry is worried sick. She didn't know what I was going to walk into once I got up here."

Cole turned off her headlights and followed her into the house. He turned on the living room lamp so she could see the dial.

"Yes, yes, he's fine. I'm fine, too." Lesley laughed at the relief in her sister's voice. "I won't be long," she promised and replaced the receiver.

Cole took her by the hand and led her into the long hall before pulling her into his arms and kissing her soundly.

Lesley looked up at him through thick lashes, her eyes warm with the effect of his touch. "Why are you kissing me here?" She glanced behind him into the narrow hallway.

Cole held her roughly against him, his chin rubbing back and forth across the crown of her head. "No windows," he muttered.

"Windows?" The word didn't make sense until she realized that they would have made an easy target standing as they were. Closing her eyes, Lesley accepted the comfort and warmth of Cole's enveloping embrace. "Have you missed me?"

"Like crazy," he whispered thickly.

"Want me to sing a few bars for you?"

"Nope." His breath felt warm against her ear as he took a small nibbling bite.

"The . . . the last time I was in your apartment you were saying something about not bothering to get new furniture because . . . because you'll be leaving soon."

"Is that what upset you?" He grew still, but his hold didn't relax.

"Yes," she admitted honestly. How could he say how desperately he missed her one minute and speak of leaving her the next?

"Would you feel any better if I explained that I have no intention of leaving Coeur d'Alene without you?"

Lesley felt as if her heart were about to explode. "You don't?"

"I had no intention of falling in love when I moved here. Love was the last thing on my mind."

"You love me, honestly love me?" Lesley cried, spreading eager kisses over his face and neck.

A hand at both sides of her face stopped her long enough for him to kiss her quiet.

"I kept telling myself it would never work, especially not now. Not at the most difficult time of my life. I couldn't drag you into this mess. But there you were dressed as a pillar of salt for a church social. I should have been laughing at you, but I don't know when I've seen anyone more desirable."

"But you left me. . . ."

"Honey, I really didn't have much choice."

"I know," she murmured, teasing his lips with fleeting kisses. "I was pretty angry with you at the time."

"Once this thing with Jennings is settled, we'll leave Coeur d'Alene and be married."

"Married?" Lesley gasped and tightened her hold on his waist. "Oh, Cole, I love you so much."

"The hardest thing I've ever done is keep my hands off you. This is going to be a short engagement."

"Very short," she agreed.

"We'll fly into Boston so you can meet my parents."

"And then to Arizona so you can meet mine," Lesley added.

"And be married as soon afterward as possible."

"I'm not going to argue."

"The money I earn from the air bag invention will be enough to set us up for a lifetime. But it might be a good idea to set some of it aside in a trust fund for our children."

"Children?" Lesley repeated. "You do move quickly, don't you? I'm just getting used to the idea of being a wife and you've already made me a mother."

"We'll build a magnificent house on a lake."

Lesley laid her head against his chest, hardly able to take in everything he was saying. "This is getting better all the time."

"With a soundproof room for you to sing in."

Tipping her head back, Lesley laughed into eyes that were warm and shining with that special loving glow. For the first time she was looking at Cole and seeing past the pain and bitterness that had haunted him all these weeks. "I should be angry at that remark, but I'm too much in love to care."

"I didn't feel I had the right to ask you to share my life until I heard from Lansky, but I need you. My whole life can be in turmoil, but as long as you're by my side nothing else matters."

"That's the way I feel."

"I love you, Lesley Brown."

"And I love you, Daniel Cole Engstrom."

He continued to hold her around the waist as if he couldn't bear to release her. "Let's sit down. There's a lot we need to discuss."

A small burst of happy laughter erupted from

Lesley. "And I was so sure God had made a mistake when He moved you beside me."

Cole looked down on her, his face frowning. "How's that?"

"Terry and I'd prayed about who was going to move into the duplex. When it was you, I was sure God had made a terrible error."

"After the first week, you'd nearly convinced me I had, too," he joked.

"What made you choose this apartment?"

They sat together on the couch. Cole looped an arm around her shoulder, bringing her head to rest against his shoulder. "The lake. I'd been driving for two days, not sure where I'd stop, having more or less decided to hole up in a small eastern Washington community. But the beauty of the lake seemed to beckon me. I stopped in at a real estate office and rented the duplex sight unseen."

"But God sent you," Lesley added confidently.

Cole didn't respond for a long moment. "If you say so."

Some of Lesley's happiness was dampened by doubt at Cole's tone. "You have a hard time believing as strongly as I do about Christ, don't you?"

"It's not that I don't believe. I guess I'm more agnostic than anything."

"Do my strong feelings bother you?"

"No," he responded in a straightforward tone.

"Whatever you want is fine. The kids, too. If it's important to you, I'll go to church and the whole bit, but only because I love you."

Lesley vacillated. It was important to her—more than important: vital. Her relationship with Jesus had priority over everything in her life, including Cole. The thought flitted through her mind that if he agreed to come to church with her, she couldn't really expect more. Not for now anyway. That he was open-minded and willing was all she needed.

The phone rang, and Lesley could feel Cole tense at her side.

"It could be Terry," Lesley murmured reassuringly.

"Or Lansky," Cole added.

She watched his face as he picked up the receiver. "Yes." The lone word sounded clipped and final.

A play of emotions showed in his face. He looked for a moment as if someone had kicked him in the stomach.

Automatically Lesley reached for his hand, squeezing it. She was shocked at how cold it was. She watched as Cole went completely white, his face devoid of color as he laid down the phone.

"What is it?"

He looked at her, and she saw again the intensity with which he hated. "Lansky." His words were barely audible. "I know why Jennings didn't kill me when he had the chance."

"Why?"

"He didn't need to. The patent had already been awarded."

"Cole," she pleaded, "you're speaking in riddles. Tell me what happened."

"Jennings was awarded the patent," he said in a voice that was devoid of emotion. He sat and buried his face in his hands.

Chapter Nine

Lesley closed her eyes as the hurt and dis-appointment for Cole curled around her, cutting off her voice for a stunned moment. "Oh, Cole," she whispered, "I'm so sorry. Is there anything that can be done?"

He raised his head and looked straight ahead. "Not now, not legally anyway."

Just the way he said it shot a shiver of cold fear up Lesley's back. "Cole, what are you going to do?"

"Ruin Jennings," he replied without the least hesitation.

"And yourself in the process." Her voice was high-pitched, with a sharp edge of fear.

"Listen, Lesley, let's get one thing straight right now. My business life is my own. I do what I want, when I want. If you're going to be my wife, that's something you'll have to accept here and now."

"I don't understand." Her fingers were laced together until she was sure the fierce grip had cut off the flow of blood to her hands.

"Understand?" he repeated angrily. "What's so difficult about it?"

"Okay," Lesley murmured in a trembling breath, "maybe you'd better define what it is you want from a wife."

"A home." He sounded determined.

"Wouldn't a housekeeper serve as well?" How could she argue with Cole. He'd just heard the most devastating news of his life and she was fighting with him over a definition. "Cole." She said his name softly, not revealing any of her own anger and disappointment. "I'm sorry. These are the kinds of questions we can discuss later. For now we've got to trust God to see that justice is done."

"Trust God?" Cole spat the words back with bitter rejection. "God is righteous and just? Then I would have been awarded the patent."

Lesley placed her hands over her ears, unable to bear hearing his hostility. "Cole, please, don't say that. I know you're angry. You have every right to be. But there's a reason for this. God wouldn't have allowed it to happen otherwise."

"I'm being cheated out of millions of dollars. Doesn't that mean anything to you? We could have been set for life—no problems, no worries."

"Of course it matters. Not the money so much as the fact you deserve to have been awarded the patent."

"I might have won if they—Jennings' men—hadn't found the car."

"The car?"

"I had a prototype of the air bag installed in a sports car. I gave it to Lansky because he felt it was the evidence we needed to prove my case. But Jennings' men destroyed it. Apparently inside they found my road map and evidence that I stopped in Coeur d'Alene."

Lesley had wondered about the red car he had driven when he first arrived. Now she knew.

"Cole," she murmured and laid her hand over his. "Let's sleep on this. It's been a blow, a terrible blow. You have every right to be angry and disappointed. I'll go back to Terry's and spend the night there. But tomorrow I'll be home and we can discuss things then."

He nodded, but Lesley wasn't sure he'd even heard what she'd said.

He walked her to the door. Lesley turned and wrapped her arms around him, allowing her love to flow from her as she murmured a silent prayer on his behalf. Cole crushed her to him and buried his face in her neck while he drew in deep, shuddering breaths.

"Do you want me to stay?" she asked in a low, gentle voice when he didn't release her.

He raised his face until their gazes met. The dark, haunted look in his eyes pulled at her heart. "No, I think I'd rather be alone, at least for a little while. There are some things I need to sort out within myself."

"Tomorrow's Thanksgiving. I'll be here early."

"Okay." His look was as absent as his word.

Lesley didn't sleep, knowing Cole probably couldn't either. Now she regretted having stayed the night with Terry. Cole might need her. But he hadn't encouraged her to stay; he wanted privacy until he had worked things out in his own mind. It was well after two o'clock when Lesley fell into a deep slumber, her mind filled with troubled prayers for Cole.

"Morning, sleepyhead," Terry greeted cheerfully as Lesley stumbled into the kitchen, arms stretched high above her head as she yawned.

"My goodness, what time is it?"

"After nine."

Wiping the sleep from her eyes, Lesley walked across the small room and poured herself a cup of coffee. "I don't suppose that was Cole on the phone?" The ring had wakened her.

"No, one of Robert's cousins. They're coming for dinner."

"I hope you won't be offended if I spend the day with Cole." Lesley had been too exhausted and mentally drained to tell her sister Lansky's news when she returned the night before.

"Why not bring him along? There's always room for one more."

171

"I . . . I don't think so. Not this time. Cole got word yesterday that he lost the patent, so he's not in any mood to socialize."

"Oh, Lesley," Terry groaned. "How awful for him."

"He's not taking it well."

"Who can blame him? He's being cheated out of years of work. Isn't there anything anyone can do?"

"Apparently not, but I don't think that's going to stop Cole from trying." Lesley pulled out the kitchen chair and sat, her hands supporting her head. Already a faint throbbing ache had begun. "It sounds crazy, but you know what Bible story kept running through my mind last night?"

Terry looked up expectantly. "No?"

"About Joseph. Remember how his brothers sold him into slavery and then he became Potiphar's trusted servant in Egypt."

"Until Potiphar's wife wanted to seduce him."

"But when Joseph refused, Potiphar's wife went running to her husband with terrible lies about Joseph, and Joseph was sent to prison."

"Unjustly," Terry added with a curt nod.

"Yes, but even in those horrible conditions Joseph cared about others; his spirit was never broken."

Terry pulled up a chair and sat across from Lesley. "What are you saying?"

Lesley wasn't sure herself, or even why the story had stuck so prominently in her mind. She saw Cole at a crossroads of his life. This whole thing with Jennings would make him either bitter or better, make or break him. But unlike Joseph, Cole didn't have a strong faith. Lesley's greatest fear was that Cole's spirit would be broken. "I love Cole." Her smile was wan as she lowered her gaze to the steaming coffee.

"I guessed as much. Is the feeling mutual?"

Lesley's hand tightened around the mug handle. "Cole asked me to marry him yesterday, and I agreed."

"That's wonderful news." Terry's voice seemed to contain the same reservations Lesley was feeling.

"It should be, but Cole asked me before he received word from his attorney. He was so different afterward. I don't know how he feels now, and I'm almost afraid to ask."

"If he honestly loves you, then it won't make any difference. Give him time," Terry advised. "He's only just heard the news. And give yourself time. Marriage is a serious commitment."

"I realize that," Lesley admitted, biting into the corner of her bottom lip. "I'm not so concerned for myself as for Cole. I'm afraid he's going to do something stupid."

"You're not going to feel right until you see and talk to him. So get dressed and get moving.

And for goodness' sake, don't tell him the story of Joseph and Potiphar's wife. He won't be in any mood to hear it."

Lesley laughed lightly, but recognized the wisdom of her sister's words.

Cole opened the front door and greeted her with a fierce hug.

"How'd you sleep?" she asked. The question was silly. He wore the same clothes as yesterday and looked as if he hadn't gone to bed. Shadows darkened his cheeks, and the frown that drove deep grooves into his forehead appeared to be permanent.

"I didn't. What about you?"

Lesley shook her head, silently confirming she had slept no better.

"I talked to Lansky again after you left. There's a chance."

"But you said . . ."

"I haven't got time to explain. I'm catching the first plane out of Spokane."

Lesley felt her heart drop to her knees. For the first time she noticed the packed suitcases standing in the living room. Had he even planned to tell her he was leaving? Her gaze narrowed on the bags, and she must have looked as shocked as she felt.

"Honey, I was sincere about everything I said yesterday. You and I were meant to be together.

You're the only good thing that's ever happened to me. I'm going after Jennings for us."

"But I don't want our marriage to start like this."

"Don't you understand?" Cole returned, and rubbed a weary hand over his tired face. "I'm doing this for our future."

"The only future I want is with you, but I don't need the fancy house on the lake and the huge trust funds for our children."

Cole knotted his hands at his side, his temper obviously on a short string. "But *I* need the house, the trust funds, the money. I earned them and I'm going to have them."

Lesley couldn't argue. He had done exactly as he said, and by all rights the money should be his.

"I'll drive you to the airport," she offered in a low, defeated voice. "How long do you think you'll be gone?"

Lovingly Cole gripped her shoulders and kissed her forehead. "I'll be back as soon as possible. Believe me, I don't want to stay away any longer than necessary. I want to see us married, settled and starting a family."

His words of promise rang in her ears as she stood in the Spokane airport and waved to his departing plane, a smile frozen on her lips. Tears filled her eyes and flowed heedlessly down pale cheeks as his plane ascended into the clear November sky.

• • •

The sights and sounds of Christmas filled the air. Lesley and Terry had volunteered to be in charge of the church Christmas program and worked long hours on the planned pageant. Although Lesley found it difficult to maintain her usual Christmas spirit, working with the children helped fill her time and keep her from worrying about Cole.

Although he phoned daily, Lesley hadn't seen him since Thanksgiving and her watery farewell in Spokane.

Following his attorney's advice, Cole had appealed the patent decision and was struggling to come up with the necessary evidence to prove his case. The patent and the appeal filled his life. Some days Lesley wondered why he bothered to phone her. He seemed to be living in another world, one far removed from her life in Coeur d'Alene.

As Christmas approached, he repeatedly promised to come to Coeur d'Alene for a visit. Every night she prayed fervently that he would. She was hungry for the sight of him and almost desperate to know that the love between them was as real to Cole as it was to her.

The Christmas program was scheduled for the Sunday school hour the morning of the twentieth of December. Like typical stage mothers, Lesley and Terry made sure every detail was as perfect as possible.

Everything ran smoothly, and over dinner at Terry's afterward they discussed the amusing antics of the cast.

"Did you see Jamie Lowell peek at the audience from inside the camel costume?" Terry asked, laughter dancing in her bright blue eyes. "I thought I'd scream."

"You did," Lesley reminded her. "That's what made Julie Palmer spill the gold."

"It was my opinion the three Wise Men were *men,*" Robert interrupted, sitting beside his wife and looping an arm around her shoulder.

"We ran out of boys," Terry informed him primly. "But all in all, everything went very well."

"Even if we do say so ourselves," Lesley chimed in. The three had gathered together in the living room after a meal of roast beef and Yorkshire pudding, or what Terry insisted was Yorkshire pudding. Lesley and Robert remained somewhat skeptical.

"Heard from Cole lately?" The question came with deceptive casualness from Robert.

"Every day," she replied and focused her attention on the gaily decorated Christmas tree rather than meet her brother-in-law's questioning regard.

"He's still coming for Christmas, isn't he?" Terry quizzed.

"I hope so."

"Do I detect a note of doubt?" Robert raised thick brows with the question.

Lesley shook her head lightly. "Cole claims he's coming, but I don't know how. His schedule seems impossible. He's meeting with his attorney Wednesday morning in Detroit, then flying into Spokane, weather permitting, and renting a car there."

"Thank goodness he had the common sense not to have you come get him. Not on these roads."

She'd wanted to meet him, had pleaded with him to let her drive to Spokane, but Cole had refused.

Robert and Terry were having a small Christmas gathering with Robert's parents. With road conditions so hazardous, it wasn't a time to be traveling. Lesley had also been invited to the family gathering, but had declined. She wanted to spend as much of her time with Cole as possible. He couldn't stay long and planned to fly out again on the twenty-sixth.

The phone was ringing Wednesday afternoon when Lesley walked in the door.

"Hello," she answered breathlessly.

"Hi, honey."

"Cole," she cried, dismay creeping into her voice. "Where are you?"

"Detroit."

"Detroit," she echoed, her heart sinking. She closed her eyes at the painful rush of disappointment. "You can't make it." She made the announcement for him, her voice unbelievably calm.

"Honey, I'm sorry."

A thick lump was blocking her throat. "This really is a terrible time of the year to plan on any traveling." Her voice was soft and quivering. "Jesus did have to pick the coldest month of the year to be born," she said, attempting a joke. "Did I tell you it's snowing again? All the kids in town love it. A white Christmas. Everyone's dream." She continued chattering because if she stopped she'd burst into tears.

"Lesley." Cole's voice was husky with appeal. "You know how much I want to be with you."

"Yes." Her hand bit into the telephone receiver as a fresh wave of hurt and frustration rippled through her.

"It's been over a month since we've been together—the longest month of my life."

"Mine, too," she muttered, and to her horror a sob escaped. "I've got to hang up now . . . I'm baking cookies and the timer just rang." The lie was outrageous, but she had to get off the phone before she disgraced herself further. Cole's disappointment was as keen as her own, so listening to her tears wouldn't make it any easier on him.

"Lesley, I love you. Don't ever doubt that, not for a minute."

"No, of course not. Good-bye, Cole. And merry Christmas." Her hand covered her mouth as she attempted to hold back the sobs. The drone continued as she replaced the telephone, her hand gripping the handle until her fingers ached.

The bank closed at noon Christmas Eve. If Terry knew about Cole's call, she'd insist Lesley come with them to Robert's parents. But their plans for the holidays were already set, and Lesley preferred not to intrude on the family gathering. In the light of Cole's call she wasn't in a celebrating mood and decided to spend the time alone.

The soft Christmas music from the record player helped to lighten her mood as she fixed herself a special dinner of chicken cordon bleu and fresh spinach salad. The small Christmas tree was decorated with a hundred starched snowflakes she had crocheted in lace. The few presents her parents had mailed, and the one Terry delivered the day before, were stacked under the tree beside the one she had for Cole.

The inspiring notes of the *Messiah* filled the small duplex. Lesley hummed as she washed her dinner dishes, then sat with her feet propped up on the coffee table, her eyes closed. The music satisfied her loneliness.

The pounding on the front door nearly caused her to fall off the couch. Christmas Eve. Who would possibly be out this time of night? Her eyes flew to her wristwatch. It was after eleven.

"Lesley," the dear, familiar male voice shouted. Cole. Her heart somersaulted as she rushed to the front door. "Cole!" Her arms flew around his neck and she spread a multitude of tiny kisses over his face. "You're here, you're here," she repeated again and again, her joy overflowing. "You must be freezing," she murmured and lovingly held his face with her hands. "Come inside."

He pounded the snow off his boots and followed her into the duplex. She watched him as he removed his thick coat and scarf. His face was red with the cold, his hair wet from the snow, but he looked marvelous . . . wonderful.

"Sit down, and let me get you something warm to drink. Are you hungry?" She took his coat and hung it where it would dry.

"The only thing I need to warm me is you." His arm crept around her waist and pulled her onto his lap. "It's good to see you, woman." Smiling, he wiped the moist tears of happiness from her cheek. For a breathless moment they looked at each other. It had been almost a month since he'd held her, touched her. Lesley had often wondered what she'd feel when she saw Cole again. Everything had happened so fast after he'd heard from Lansky. His declaration of love, his proposal seemed so distant.

"You really are beautiful, Lesley Brown," he whispered as his mouth settled hungrily over hers. Boundless joy raced through her as she gave herself freely to the mastery of his kiss.

Long moments later, her head resting against his broad shoulder, Lesley breathed in the fresh scent of woodsy after-shave and the tangy hint of spice. "How'd you get here?" Nothing mattered now that he was here and in her arms.

"The airport cleared enough for my flight to take off, but we were forced to land in Salt Lake City because of a new storm front. I would have phoned, but I didn't want you worrying and wondering."

"Cole, I wish you had."

"Sometime early this morning we landed in Seattle and I drove from there."

"Seattle!" she gasped. "That's a good nine hours' drive."

"Twelve. Snoqualmie Pass was closed for two hours because of a snowslide."

Keeping her arm around his shoulder, she raised her face enough so that they could look at each other. "You went through all that trouble to get to me?"

"Nothing was more important than making it here for Christmas."

The warmth of his hold burned through Lesley's thin sweater. A rawness caught in her throat at the thought of what he had endured for her. "You do love me, don't you?"

"Had you begun to doubt it?"

"In some ways I think I had," she admitted in low tones.

"But not anymore?"

"Never again." Tenderly her fingertips traced the proud, determined line of his jaw. Cole was like that. When he wanted something, he was relentless until satisfied. Every day she prayed that the ordeal with the patent would be settled, because she didn't know if Cole would rest until it was.

"Are you ready to open your present?" he asked in a husky murmur as his teeth made biting kisses along the lobe of her ear.

"You brought me a gift?" He hadn't been carrying anything.

"Here." He reached inside his jacket pocket and handed her a small jeweler's box. "I didn't have time to wrap it."

"Cole, you didn't?" From the box size it wasn't difficult to guess what was inside.

"I would have preferred to have us shop for your ring together, but I thought, circumstances being what they are, you'd understand."

Slowly she opened the lid of the plush black velvet box. A huge solitaire diamond sparkled back at her. Lesley drew in a gasp of delight. "It's beautiful," she whispered, her breath stuck in her throat. "It's perfect. I couldn't have chosen anything more beautiful."

"Let's try it on for size." He took the ring out of the holder and slipped it onto her finger, the fit as perfect as the diamond.

Holding her left hand out for them both to examine, Lesley felt a sense of awe come over her. Cole's declaration of love, the proposal and all it entailed seemed real to her now.

"Since you're an engaged woman, it's about time you had a ring to prove it, wouldn't you say?"

"Yes." Lesley beamed happily. "Yes, I would."

Cole's restless hand moved caressingly up and down her spine. "I'd like to set a wedding date, but I want this thing settled with Jennings first."

Lesley swallowed at the building tightness in her throat. "How much longer?"

A look of pain flashed across his face. Now, after the first moments of shock at his arrival, Lesley could study him more closely. He looked tired, but the weariness was more than physical. Losing the patent had taken its toll, had planted bitter seeds in his heart and mind. He'd lost weight; his face was thin, almost gaunt. His cheekbones were pronounced, and tiny lines fanned out from his eyes. His thick dark hair, needing to be trimmed, covered the back of his collar. His all-consuming drive was leading to physical neglect.

"I don't know how much longer." He raked a hand along the side of his head.

"A month, maybe two?" Lesley quizzed, praying it wouldn't be any more time than that. "A girl likes to know these things."

He kissed the tip of her nose. "By summer for sure."

"Summer," she gasped, doing her best to disguise her disappointment. "Cole," she said softly, not looking at him as she spoke, "would it be so unreasonable to leave the past buried and go on with our lives?"

"Yes," he answered forcefully. "The hearing for the appeal is scheduled the second week in January. Let's decide what to do after that?"

"Okay," she agreed. Maybe she was being selfish, but their future was together and she hated these separations. "Would you like me to fix you something to eat?"

"I'm starved," he answered. "I can't remember the last time I ate."

"Honestly, Cole, sometimes I think we'd better get married now just so I'll be around to take care of you."

"Now, that's a thought." But he was teasing, and they both knew it.

She rose from his lap and looked through the refrigerator for something to cook. "How does bacon and eggs sound?"

"Marvelous," he answered on the tail of a yawn. "I'm going to lie down for a few minutes."

Lesley watched as he stretched out on the sofa and closed his eyes. She recognized that he was almost instantly asleep and wondered how long it'd been since he'd seen a bed. Gently she closed the refrigerator: there was no need to cook anything. Fifteen minutes later she spread a thick blanket over him and lovingly brushed the hair from his forehead. He looked almost childlike in slumber. Her lips lightly brushed over his as she turned out the lights and tiptoed into her own room.

"It's beautiful," Terry breathed in awe as she examined Lesley's ring. "I bet you were surprised."

Terry didn't know the half of it. "I was."

"It's too bad Cole had to leave so soon."

"So soon" was right. Lesley awoke Christmas morning to find a message on her kitchen table. He had to get back to Detroit, and after checking with the airlines he'd found the only available space was on a flight that left at eight that morning. He signed the note with his love and the promise that they would spend every Christmas the rest of their lives together.

The engagement ring felt awkward on her hand the first few days, but Lesley soon discovered that having it meant more to her than any gift she'd ever had. At least she had some physical evidence of Cole's love and commitment to her.

"Did he have any news about the patent decision?" Terry asked anxiously.

"We should know something the second week in January. Pray, Terry," Lesley pleaded. "The sooner this thing is settled, the sooner Cole and I can get on with our lives."

Never had the days of January dragged so laboriously. Lesley waited and waited. Then the decision came when she'd least expected to hear.

On January 15, Lesley was at her desk at the bank when Charlotte Lewis told her there was a call for her on line two.

"Lesley Brown," she answered in her efficient business tone.

"The appeal was denied." Cole announced in a flat voice that didn't disguise his frustration.

"No," she whispered as the meaning of what he was saying hit. "Oh, Cole." Lesley could feel the defeat and anger in his voice. But it was over, at last, and they could accept that and go on from there. "I know it's small compensation now, but at least you have the satisfaction of knowing the air bag you invented will save thousands of lives."

"Lesley, don't feed me platitudes. Not now."

She breathed in deeply. "What do you want me to say?"

There was a savage note to his voice. "I don't know."

"When will I see you again?"

He sucked in a ragged breath. "Let me sort things out here and I'll get back to you."

"Okay. I'm sorry things didn't go well. I love you," she whispered for his ears alone.

"Some days that's the only thing that keeps me going."

Lesley didn't hear from Cole for another week, one of the longest weeks of her life. Unable to contact him by phone, she wrote him long, chatty letters every night. She tried to offer assurances, but after the first few days she realized these would do little to comfort him.

The January snows melted, and February quickly turned to March and the promise of spring. Cole wired her a dozen long-stemmed red roses on Valentine's Day with a message of his love. Lesley didn't doubt his love, but she recognized that his hate for Jennings was far stronger than any of his feelings for her.

With April came Easter and the return of her parents from Arizona. Cole had told her he'd fly in the weekend her parents returned, so he could meet his future in-laws.

Lesley picked him up at the Spokane airport. When he stepped off the plane she was shocked at his appearance. His features were strikingly gaunt, his dark eyes haunted. The smile on her lips wavered as he stepped into the terminal.

Tears blurred her vision as Cole approached. He set his briefcase on the ground and hugged her fiercely, burying his face in her neck.

"I've missed you," she whispered brokenly.

"I know, love, I feel the same way." His kiss was as urgent as his embrace. He smiled into her eyes and gently brushed a tear aside. "I like your hair."

Her hand reached automatically for the short curls. She'd had it cut last month.

"You look terrible," she replied honestly and brushed an imaginary piece of lint from his suit coat.

"But I'm making progress." He placed his arm around her waist, pulling her close to his side.

"Are you?" She didn't mean to sound so unsure. Progress—but at what price?

"Only a little, I admit."

"This battle can go on for years, can't it?"

He tensed and his hand tightened around her. "I won't let that happen."

"It's already happening," she murmured. "Cole, you're killing yourself over a stupid air bag. Is it worth it? Answer me, is your life worth less than some invention?" She knew she sounded angry and unreasonable, but she couldn't stand by and say nothing. Not anymore.

Lesley could feel him withdraw. He stopped mid-stride, and although he continued to hold her, he might as well have been miles away.

"Yes," he said finally, his dark eyes stony-hard. "If I can't have justice, then I'll have my revenge, and that's worth more than anything . . . even you, Lesley."

Chapter Ten

"Even me," Lesley repeated, stunned. "Cole," she breathed, "look at what you're doing to yourself. I realize better than anyone how terrible this ordeal has been for you."

"You couldn't possibly know," he announced and savagely raked a hand through his hair.

"Maybe not," she conceded. "But I see what's happening to you. I hear the bitterness in your voice, I read the hatred in your letters. And then I look at what all this has done to you physically and I want to cry. What happened to the man who asked me to marry him? The man who wanted a home and family?"

"I still want that," Cole insisted. "But don't you understand, I'm doing this for us." His mouth was tightly pinched, and Lesley recognized that his temper was held on a taut rein.

"Then you're lying to yourself and to me."

They paused in front of the baggage carousel. Lesley centered her gaze on the variety of suitcases as they arrived instead of glancing at Cole, afraid of what his eyes would say.

190

"Nothing like this has ever happened to me," she continued, "I guess you could say I've lived a sheltered life." She felt Cole's gaze roam over her face, and turned to offer him a weak smile. "In some ways I have you to thank for one of the biggest strides I've made in my spiritual life."

"I don't understand."

Lesley had doubted that he would. "Do you remember Halloween night when I told you I was going to pray for you?"

Amusement touched his mouth and Lesley wondered how long it had been since Cole had smiled, really smiled.

"I remember."

"Later you pulled up beside my car in the ditch and told me you were going to pray for me. I can't remember a time in my life I was angrier."

He chuckled and his hand affectionately squeezed her shoulder. "I'm rather proud of that comment."

Swallowing her pride, Lesley shook her head. "You should be. It helped me see what I was becoming." At his frown she elaborated. "Until I met you I was quickly becoming a self-righteous prude."

"And I changed that?"

Hands laced in front of her, Lesley smiled absently. "You helped me see that I was becoming so heavenly-minded that I wasn't any earthly good. I've never thanked you for that. Knowing you and loving you has helped me more than I could ever explain in mere words."

"But that's what I'm trying to tell you. Your love and support have made these last months bearable. I couldn't have done it without you."

Inwardly Lesley groaned, realizing that in the most important of matters she had failed him.

Cole retrieved his suitcase, and with their hands linked they strode to the parking lot.

"You'd better tell me something about your parents," he suggested as she handed him the car keys. He unlocked her door, then walked around the front of the car and climbed into the driver's seat. "It's not every day a man meets his future in-laws."

"You don't need to worry. I think Mom and Dad are more nervous about meeting you." Her parents had arrived that Wednesday and planned a small dinner party for Cole and Lesley Saturday night. To say that her parents were curious would be an understatement.

The freeway leading from Spokane to Coeur d'Alene was particularly beautiful in the spring, when lush green contrasted with a pale blue sky. They sat not speaking, Lesley close to his side.

"Did I tell you Lansky warned me that marriage is often a three-ring circus?" Cole broke the silence.

"How's that?" Lesley looked over to him expectantly.

"First there's the engagement ring, then the wedding ring, and finally the suffering."

"Clever," she muttered, feigning indignation.

Chuckling, Cole pulled off to the side of the road and reached for her. He kissed her ardently; the hunger in him for her love was so overpowering it almost frightened Lesley.

"Why is it every minute apart is agony, and then the first chance we're together all we do is argue?" Cole asked her breathlessly, his forehead resting against hers.

"I don't know why. We're both dumb, I guess," Lesley said and rubbed her face along the slightly rough surface of his jaw in a feline action. "I love you, Cole, and it's hurting me just as much as you to be apart like this. Can't we forget Jennings?"

"I wish we could." He kissed the crown of her head and ran his fingers through the short dark curls. "No, I have to revise that. I wish I could, but I won't rest until things are set right."

Lesley released a long, slow breath, straightened and leaned her head against the back of the seat cushion.

"How's the apartment?" Cole asked, changing the subject.

"Fine." He'd kept his apartment in Coeur d'Alene and left Lesley his car, though she rarely drove it: there was little need, since she had her own vehicle.

As Coeur d'Alene Lake came into view, the faint stirrings of pride brought a sigh of contentment from Lesley. "Paul said to say hello, by the way."

"Paul?" Cole looked at her blankly.

"The grocer from Resort Grocery."

"Oh yes, Mr. Christian."

"Mr. Christian?" Now it was Lesley's turn to look confused.

"Yes. Paul used to place Bible verses in the bottom of my bags every week. I got quite a kick out of him. Nice old fellow."

"He's lived a hard life. When Paul was ready to retire and give his business to his son, they discovered Jeff had cancer. Paul mortgaged the business and spent the money on medical bills. Jeff died a year later."

"That's tough for any man."

"It was especially tough for Paul. Jeff was his only child, and they were as close as any father and son could be."

Cole was quiet as they approached the outskirts of town and turned off the familiar road that led up the hill to the duplex.

Lesley's gaze studied him as they drew closer. She loved this man, but she was losing him, might already have lost him.

"I love you," she whispered, feeling a crazy

kind of desperation, not knowing what else to say or how to express herself.

"I could never doubt that." Cole's hand found hers on the seat beside him and gently squeezed it. Keeping his eyes on the road, he raised her hand to his lips and tenderly kissed her palm. "You'd have to love me to stand these past months."

Lesley felt all her hard-fought-for poise slip away from her. She had to talk to Cole, make him see the uselessness of this thing with Jennings.

When Cole parked on his half of the driveway, Lesley told him, "I put a casserole in the oven before I left. I hope you're hungry."

"That was a very wifely thing to do," he teased her affectionately.

"I was just practicing."

"Good."

"I only have three days to fatten you up and add some color to your face, and believe me, I'm going to take advantage of every one of those days." Three glorious days; she'd waited impatiently, circling the weekend off on her calendar. She'd felt like a child on Christmas Day when she awoke that morning, knowing Cole would be arriving.

"Honey," Cole said thoughtfully, stopping her from opening her car door. "I've been meaning to say something, but I didn't want to until it was necessary."

"Necessary? What?" A feeling of dread came over her. He was here; nothing else should matter.

"I can't stay as long as we'd planned. I have to be back early Sunday morning, which means I'll have to catch the plane tomorrow night."

With forced calm, her eyes wide with shock and hurt, Lesley turned and met his gaze. His eyes were pleading with her to understand. He didn't want to leave so soon, but it was necessary.

A tightening sensation gripped the muscles of her stomach into a cold, hard knot. The pain was so intense that she couldn't speak for several seconds.

"Don't look at me like that," Cole pleaded.

Numbly Lesley shook her head. "I can't help it." She opened her car door and blindly walked into her apartment, leaving the screen door open.

Cole followed her inside.

Lesley stood in front of the sliding glass door in the kitchen, her arms cradling her stomach. Her lungs took in deep breaths of oxygen as she struggled to hold back the emotion.

"I know you're angry and I don't blame you," Cole said from behind her. Gently he placed his hands on her shoulders as if he wanted to ease the hurt but wasn't sure how.

With a trembling smile she turned to face him. "Cole, sit down. We need to talk."

His eyes met hers, and he gently brushed a curl from her forehead. "This sounds serious."

"More serious than any discussion I've ever had." She led him into the living room and sat him on the couch while she remained standing. "Do you remember what I told you about Paul?"

"Mr. Christian and his son?" His look spoke plainly of trepidation.

She paced across the floor. "Yes. I know this is going to be difficult for you to understand, but hear me out."

He attempted a grin. "Is it necessary for you to pace back and forth like that when you tell me?"

"Yes." She nodded curtly. "I'm afraid it is." Taking in a quivering breath, she continued. "Everything I've done in my life—all that I've experienced, each delight, every difficulty—has made me what I am today."

Cole looked confused.

"It's true I've never experienced great tragedy, but I've witnessed what has happened to others who have."

"The grocer."

"Yes, Paul. He's a wonderful, loving man because he has risen above the horrible pain of losing his son. There is no bitterness in his heart. When a family lost their only son in a drowning incident this summer, it was Paul who offered them comfort."

"That's understandable."

"I . . . I don't know anyone who can help you, and right now I feel terribly inadequate. I love . . .

you." She faltered slightly, then regained fluency. "And because I love you, I can see what all this hatred for Jennings is doing to you. Your bitterness and drive for revenge have become an obsession, an angry monster that's consuming your life." She stood directly in front of him. "You invented a wonderful safety device that will save thousands of lives. Unfortunately, you'll probably never get the credit. But you have the personal satisfaction of this accomplishment. Isn't it enough?"

"No," Cole shouted, his face cold and solemn, his narrowed eyes darkened with emotion. He stopped and rubbed a hand over his eyes, then the side of his face, distorting his features. "I won't rest until I've seen justice."

"That will probably never happen. You've got to accept this and a whole lot more." She paused, knowing how difficult this would be for Cole and how hard it was for her to say these things to him. "You need peace within yourself. You've got to forgive Jennings."

"Forgive Jennings!" Cole spat in disbelief. "You're crazy."

"I've never been more serious in my life."

"Then you couldn't possibly understand what that man has done to me," Cole shouted. "To us."

"What Jennings did was wrong," she replied calmly. "I could never deny that. But what you're doing to yourself is far worse."

Cole bound to his feet and stalked to one end of the room, his eyes blazing. "I can't believe you'd even suggest such a thing."

The smile that touched her eyes was troubled and sad. "It's the way I was raised. My parents brought up Terry and me in an atmosphere of love and forgiveness. We were raised in the church—"

"Here it comes." The shadows of pain darkened his eyes. "I thought you just got done telling me I'd helped you get over being a self-righteous prude?"

"That doesn't have anything to do with this," Lesley defended herself, looking straight into Cole's shocked expression.

"But you're going to give me some holier-than-thou advice about forgiving the man who's ruining my life."

"The man you're letting ruin your life," she amended, hoping he would catch the subtle difference.

"Lesley, listen to me," Cole pleaded, fighting for control of his temper. "You're not making any sense."

With an aching heart, Lesley studied Cole: the roughly carved jaw, the thick creased grooves in his forehead, the tight line of his mouth. She would give anything to make herself clear, anything to help him understand.

"Today is Good Friday," she said at last.

A heavy silence hung in the room.

"What's that supposed to mean to me?" His expression was as hard as a granite wall.

"Unless you're a Christian, I guess it doesn't mean much."

"Then why bring it into the conversation now?" Slowly he walked to the far side of the room, his hard gaze pinning her.

"Because we were talking about forgiveness."

"Are we back on that subject again?"

Lesley's smile was tremulous. "I never stopped talking about it. When Jesus hung on that cross, He wasn't the pretty picture some artists have depicted. He was beaten so badly that he was unrecognizable as a man. He hung in shame between two criminals."

"Are you going to insist on giving me a Bible lesson?"

"Yes," she cried, her voice shaking violently. "Yes, I am, because maybe then you'll understand. Jesus was perfect . . . sinless . . . the Lamb of God."

Cole glanced away, a bored look on his face.

"When Jesus hung on the cross, He took every sin, every evil that was ever in the world—the past, the present and the future. He became so hideously ugly with sin that God the Father had to actually turn His back on Him. That was why Jesus called out and asked why His Father had forsaken Him."

"How much more of this do I have to listen to?"

"Not much."

His look was one of indulgent cynicism. "Good." He crossed his arms in front of his chest as if that could block out her words.

"Yet Jesus, in all his pain and torment, asked that God forgive." Lesley knew she wasn't reaching Cole, she doubted that anything she said would. Nonetheless she continued. "Don't you understand? If Jesus could show that kind of forgiveness for you and me, couldn't you find it in your heart to forgive Jennings?"

Cole's hands knotted into tight fists. For a long time he said nothing as he stood before her. He was so tall and hard, he might as well have been carved out of stone. "You ask too much."

Her eyes wide and shimmering with tears, Lesley slipped the engagement ring off her finger. "I love you, Cole, but my love will never be enough for you." She placed the ring in the palm of his hand.

"You don't mean this?" Cole's voice was as cold as the arctic wind.

"I've never been more serious."

"I won't come back." Cole's low words weren't a threat but a promise.

"I know that," she murmured and glanced down at the carpet. "God go with you, Cole."

One dark brow shot up with sardonic disbelief. "I'm taking the car with me. I'll contact the owner about the duplex. Whatever's inside can be given to charity. That's about as Christian as I plan to get." He walked out of the house, looking back at her once, his gaze whip-sharp. "Goodbye, Lesley."

A hand over her mouth to hold back the threatening sobs, Lesley watched as he walked out of her half of the house and into his half. Not questioning her actions, she took the small devotional Bible on the end table and ran outside. If she tried to give it to Cole now, he'd throw it back at her. Carefully and as noiselessly as possible she placed it in the backseat of his car.

She was in the house by the time he returned. He glanced back at her once, his look uncompromisingly hard. Without another word he backed out of the driveway and out of her life.

Chapter Eleven

"Are you all right?" Terry asked as they walked down the church corridor from the Sunday school classroom to the sanctuary. Their footsteps echoed through the long hall.

"Why shouldn't I be fine?" Lesley decided to be obtuse. Three weeks and not a word from Cole. Not that she expected him to contact her.

"Don't play dumb," Terry hissed. "You're miserable, so admit it."

"Okay, you win," Lesley answered sharply. "I'm miserable. Does that make you happy?"

"No," Terry observed softly. "It makes me as brokenhearted as you."

"Well, don't be," Lesley responded in a falsely cheerful voice. "My relationship with Cole was doomed anyway. I only hastened the process."

"But you still love him."

Fresh pain burned through her heart. "That hasn't changed, but after my speech on God's love and forgiveness, I've got to look on the positive side of this situation and grow from it."

"Don't try so hard." Her sister squeezed her arm affectionately. "Give yourself time."

Lesley arched delicately shaped brows. "Time," she said with a sigh, "the great healer." But how much time would it take for the haunting memories to dissipate? How long would it be before thoughts of Cole didn't dominate every waking minute and before her life had order again?

Every time the phone rang, her heart pounded like a jackhammer. When she checked the mailbox, her fingers shook. Cole had written and phoned her so often. And now there was nothing. Nothing. Lesley was left to pick up the pieces of her life and go on. Although she accepted the fact Cole wasn't coming back, her heart waged its own battle. Time, she had to believe, would convince her heart, too.

"Is the other half of the duplex rented?" Terry whispered as they entered the vestibule.

"Not yet." The FOR RENT sign in the grass outside the duplex was a constant reminder that Cole was gone for good.

"Any nibbles?"

Lesley shrugged. "Not that I know of."

They slipped into the pew and waited for the morning worship service to begin. Robert joined them a minute later. Lesley bowed her head, seeking to clear her thoughts and prepare her heart for the pastor's message. As she raised her head, her gaze fell on her ringless left hand. Inadvertently she touched her bare finger. She felt naked without the engagement ring.

Terry's hand reached over and squeezed hers. "You're going to make it."

Lesley nodded. Yes, she would. She'd never stop loving Cole, her heart had decreed as much. But she would be stronger, better, because of that love.

The bright spring sunshine greeted Lesley as she drove home from work Monday afternoon. The time had come to get busy in the garden. She hadn't felt like working outside. The energy spent smiling and putting on a friendly façade drained her by the end of the long workday. She usually ate a light meal, read and went to bed early. Not that she could fall asleep so quickly.

The first thing Lesley noted when she pulled into the driveway was that the FOR RENT sign had been removed from the lawn. Apparently she was going to have a new neighbor. The place had been vacant for months with Cole gone so much of the time. It would be good to have someone close again.

Pouring herself a glass of iced tea, Lesley took a long swallow and set the tall glass on the kitchen table. The jeans she wore to work in the yard were a little large in the waist, prompting her to grab a couple of cookies from the cookie jar. They tasted stale, and after one bite she tossed them both in the garbage. Saturday she'd remember to pick up a fresh supply.

The sweat shirt was a faded red one she'd had since her college days. Lesley pushed the long sleeves up past her elbows as she walked out the sliding glass door into the backyard. The garden fork was resting against the back wall of the work shed. She successfully stifled a wince when she reached for it, refusing to look at the snow shovel, which forcefully reminded her of Cole and the fun they'd had in the first snowstorm of the season.

The earth was damp, which made the tilling easier. Lesley had finished the first long row of the garden when she paused to wipe the perspiration from her brow with the back of her hand.

She stopped in mid-action as she caught a glimpse of her new neighbor. It felt as if her heart had stopped beating, and all the color drained from her face. Cole. What was he doing back? Had he forgotten something? Had he come to torment her?

He stood framed in the doorway, watching her. Their eyes clashed, shocked sparkling blue against warm velvet brown. Mesmerized, Lesley watched as he pulled open the sliding door and stepped outside.

"Hello, Lesley." He was dressed in brown slacks and a tan sweater, looking so handsome it was almost impossible for her to breath evenly.

"Hello," she managed at last.

"I take it you're surprised to see me?"

Her hand curled around the rough wood handle of the garden fork. "Yes," she whispered. She wasn't ready for a confrontation with Cole. She needed more time to prepare, to school her reactions.

"You look well."

"I'm fine." How could they exchange pleasantries like polite strangers? This was the man she loved, and all that emotion had to be shining from her eyes for him to see. Why was he standing there? "How have you been?" she asked, her voice husky.

He shrugged one muscular shoulder. "Much better, actually."

"Good." She cast her eyes down at the partially tilled garden. "As you can see, I'm at it again." The toe of her tennis shoe parted the rich soil.

"Yes, I can." His smile was strangely enigmatic.

Lesley's nerves were pulled taut until they grated against one another. "What are you doing here?" she demanded, her voice quivering violently.

"You put the Bible in the back of my car, didn't you?" He answered her question with one of his own.

"Yes." She wouldn't lie. "I knew that I couldn't help you, but I thought my Bible might."

"You're wrong, I didn't appreciate it when I found it. The fact is, I went to throw it away. Purging my life of anything that had to do with you made sense at the time."

Lesley blanched. Tossing her Bible in the garbage would be like throwing away part of herself. But apparently that had been Cole's intention.

"This fell out of it." He handed Lesley a paper she'd used to mark her place.

Lovingly she fingered the long marker and nodded. "Thank you for returning it."

"There were other things inside the cover, too." His look was unreadable.

Briefly she nodded, unable to look at him.

"The card I sent with the Valentine roses, a death announcement. Some relative?"

Again she acknowledged him with a nod of her head.

"This book is important to you."

"Yes." She'd missed it terribly, and although she'd replaced it immediately after he'd left, Lesley had had difficulty finding familiar verses. The pages were still so new they stuck together, and the leather binding remained stiff.

"As soon as I saw the treasures you had stored in its flap, I couldn't understand why you'd given it to me, but I decided maybe I couldn't throw it away."

Lesley released an unconscious sigh of relief.

"But I wasn't about to return it personally, I'd already made myself perfectly clear. I wasn't coming back to Coeur d'Alene. I meant to mail it. Instead I found myself leafing through the pages. Soon I found myself reading the Gospels. You had several verses underlined in John. 'I have come that you might have life and might have it abundantly' was one that sticks out in my mind."

"John 10:10," she supplied.

"But Jesus wasn't talking about riches, was He?"

"No, He was talking about the quality of our earthly life." Her gaze slid to him again. A beautiful feeling of hope began to mount within her.

"Soon I found verses everywhere that spoke of forgiveness: Hebrews, Psalms, Acts. I read about the new life, the abundant life. For the first time in nearly a year I slept peacefully and uninterruptedly. I have peace within myself now. I can't say that everything's behind me yet. The hate and bitterness are lessening. I haven't forgiven Jennings for what he did. But I'm willing to try, with God's help."

Lesley stood immobile for only a moment.

"I love you, Lesley. You're the best thing that's ever happened to me. I want to share this new abundant life with you. Can we start again? Can we place the past behind us?"

The garden fork fell unheeded to the damp earth as she walked to Cole and slipped her arms around his neck. Brilliant tears of happiness shimmered in her eyes as she smiled up at him.

Very gently, Cole wrapped his arms around her, and kissed her with a fierce kind of tenderness. He released a shuddering sigh as he held her close, his lips moving back and forth against the side of her head, his breath ruffling her hair.

A happiness unlike anything she'd ever experienced stole through her. "Did the landlord explain about the water pressure?" she asked teasingly.

"No," Cole murmured and brushed the hair from her cheek. "But he had plenty to say about the occupant in the second half of the duplex. Apparently my new neighbor is a karate expert."

Laughter tumbled from Lesley as she tilted her head back to gaze into the powerful face of the man she loved, the man God had sent to her.

Six months later, Lesley came in the back door of her Detroit home and placed the two grocery sacks on the kitchen counter top. Pausing, she unzipped her short jacket and tossed it across the back of the kitchen chair.

A package of cookies was on top of the first sack. She opened it and dumped them in a red apple-shaped cookie jar, nibbling on one as she put the frozen foods in the freezer section of the refrigerator.

The sounds of Cole working in the basement brought a sigh of contentment from slightly parted lips. Even after several months of marriage, her husband's genius had the ability to amaze her. His work area was a collage of ideas. Most of his work centered on the automobile and parts she hadn't known existed. But his inventions extended into the kitchen, and he had her testing a few of his crazy ideas. If she wasn't so much in love, she would have complained.

"Cole." She pushed the button of the intercom. "Would you like me to bring you down a cup of coffee?"

"Sure." He sounded preoccupied, but then he usually did when he was in his workroom.

While she finished unpacking the groceries, Lesley plugged in the coffeepot. Ten minutes later she carried two steaming cups down the stairs.

"I hope you're ready for a break."

"In just a minute," Cole answered without looking up, keenly concentrating on his latest contraption.

A smile touched the corners of her soft mouth. She'd sat an hour waiting for his "just a minute" on more than one occasion.

"Cole," she said softly, "I've got something important to tell you."

"Go ahead, I'm listening."

Lesley rolled her eyes and sighed. "I was just thinking that maybe it would be a good idea for you to start working on a new type of car seat for the baby. I was looking at ones in the shopping center today, and they don't look all that secure. Do you think you might have a couple of ideas?"

"Sure," he mumbled, "no problem."

Lesley sat on a tall stool and took a sip of her coffee. Glancing at her wristwatch, she mentally calculated how long it would take to get a reaction. Five minutes, she guessed.

"Baby!" Cole exploded, and banged his head on the light fixture as he stood up abruptly.

Lesley shot a glance at her watch. "Very good. That only took you two and a half minutes."

Rubbing the back of his head, Cole looked at her and shook his head. "Did I hear you right?"

"As a matter of fact, I think you heard me perfectly." Lesley was loving this.

"A baby? So soon? Are you sure?"

"I saw the doctor this morning."

Cole took the coffee out of her hand and set it aside. He sat on the stool beside her, his hand tenderly resting against her flat abdomen. "Why didn't you say something earlier?"

Lesley brushed the hair from his forehead. "I wanted to be certain."

"But, honey, I wanted to build you that dream home on the lake before we started a family. I want to give you diamonds and smother you in furs."

Linking her arms around his neck, Lesley pressed an ardent kiss over his mouth. "Don't you know I'm already the richest lady in town?"

Center Point Large Print
600 Brooks Road / PO Box 1
Thorndike ME 04986-0001 USA

(207) 568-3717

US & Canada:
1 800 929-9108
www.centerpointlargeprint.com